THE MAN . . . BENT FORWARD AND GLUED HIS LIPS TO

THE NOVELS, STORIES
AND SKETCHES OF
F. HOPKINSON SMITH

A WHITE UMBRELLA
IN MEXICO ❧ ❧ ❧
AND OTHER LANDS ❧

CHARLES SCRIBNER'S
SONS ❧ NEW YORK ❧ 1902

*Published under special arrangement
with Houghton, Mifflin & Co.*

I dedicate this book to the most charming of all the señoritas I know; the one whose face lingers longest in my memory while I am away, and whose arms open widest when I return; the most patient of my listeners, the most generous of my critics — my little daughter MARION.

CONTENTS

vii

CONTENTS

ILLUSTRATIONS

A WHITE UMBRELLA IN MEXICO

INTRODUCTION

M Y probe has not gone very far below the surface. The task would have been uncongenial and the result superfluous. The record of the resources, religions, politics, governments, social conditions, and misfortunes of Mexico already enlarges many folios and lies heavy on many shelves, and I hope on some consciences.

I have preferred rather to present what would appeal to the painter and idler. A land of white sunshine redolent with flowers ; a land of gay costumes, crumbling churches, and old convents ; a land of kindly greetings, of extreme courtesy, of open, broad hospitality.

I have delighted my soul with the swaying of the lilies in the sunlight, the rush of the roses crowding over mouldy walls, the broad-leaved palms cooling the shadows, and have wasted none of my precious time searching for the lizard and the mole crawling at their roots.

Content with the novelty and charm of the picturesque life about me, I have watched the

3

naked children at play and the patient peon at work; and the haughty hidalgo, armed and guarded, inspecting his plantation; and the dark-skinned señorita with her lips pressed close to the gratings of the confessional; and even the stealthy, furtive glance of the outlaw, without caring to analyze or solve any one of the many social and religious problems which make these conditions possible.

It was enough for me to find the wild life of the Comanche, the grand estate of the Spanish Don, and the fragments of the past splendor of the ecclesiastical orders existing side by side with the remnant of that Aztec civilization which fired the Spanish heart in the old days of the Conquest. Enough to discover that in this remnant there still survived a race capable of the highest culture and worthy of the deepest study. A distinct and peculiar people. An unselfish, patient, tender-hearted people, of great personal beauty, courage, and refinement. A people maintaining in their every-day life an etiquette phenomenal in a down-trodden race; offering instantly to the stranger and wayfarer on the very threshold of their adobe huts a hospitality so generous, accompanied by a courtesy so exquisite, that one stops at the next doorway to reënjoy the luxury.

4

INTRODUCTION

It was more than enough to revel in an Italian sun lighting up a semi-tropical land ; to look up to white-capped peaks towering into the blue ; to look down upon wind-swept plains encircled by ragged chains of mountains ; to catch the sparkle of miniature cities jewelled here and there in oases of olive and orange ; and to realize that to-day, in its varied scenery, costumes, architecture, street life, canals crowded with flower - laden boats, market plazas thronged with gayly dressed natives, faded church interiors, and abandoned convents, Mexico is the most marvellously picturesque country under the sun. A tropical Venice ! a semi-barbarous Spain ! a new Holy Land.

To study and enjoy this or any other people thoroughly, one must live in the streets. A chat with the old woman selling rosaries near the door of the cathredral, half an hour spent with the sacristan after morning mass, and a word now and then with the donkey-boy, the water-carrier, and the padre, will give you a better idea of a town and a closer insight into its inner life than days spent at the governor's palace or the museum.

If your companion is a white umbrella, and if beneath its shelter you sit for hours painting the picturesque bits that charm your eye, you will have hosts of lookers-on attracted by idle curiosity. Many of these will prove good friends during your stay, and will vie with each other in doing you many little acts of kindness which will linger lovingly in your memory long after you have shaken the white dust of their villages from your feet.

It is in this spirit and with this intent that I ask you to turn aside from the heat and bustle of your daily life long enough to share with me the cool and quiet of my white umbrella while it is opened in Mexico.

F. H. S.

New York, December, 1888.

I

A MORNING IN GUANAJUATO

THIS morning I am wandering about Guanajuato. It is a grotesque, quaint, old mining town, near the line of the Mexican Central Railroad, within a day's journey of the City of Mexico. I had arrived the night before, tired out, and awoke so early that the sun and I appeared on the streets about the same hour.

The air was deliciously cool and fragrant, and shouldering my sketch-trap and umbrella I bent my steps towards the church of *la parróquia*.

I had seen it the night previous as I passed by in the starlight, and its stone pillars and twisted iron railings so delighted me that I spent half the night elaborating its details in my sleep.

The tide of worshippers filling the streets carried prayer-books and rosaries. They were evidently intent on early mass. As for myself, I was simply drifting about, watching the people, making notes in my sketch-book, and saturating myself with the charming novelty of my surroundings.

7

When I reached the small square facing the great green door of the beautiful old church, the golden sunlight was just touching its quaint towers, and the stone urns and crosses surmounting the curious pillars below were still in shadow, standing out in dark relief against the blue sky beyond.

I mingled with the crowd, followed into the church, listened a while to the service, and then returned to the plaza and began a circuit of the square that I might select some point of sight from which I could seize the noble pile as a whole, and thus express it within the square of my canvas.

The oftener I walked around it, the more difficult became the problem. A dozen times I made the circuit, stopping, pondering, and stepping backwards and sideways after the manner of painters similarly perplexed; attracting a curious throng, who kept their eyes upon me very much as if they suspected I was either slightly crazed or was about to indulge in some kind of heathen rite entirely new to them.

Finally it became plainly evident that but one point of sight could be relied upon. This centred in the archway of a private house immediately opposite the church. I determined to move in and take possession.

8

Some care, however, is necessary in the inroads one makes upon a private house in a Spanish city. A watchful porter half concealed in the garden of the patio generally has his eye on the gateway, and overhauls you before you have taken a dozen steps with a *" Hola, señor ! á quién busca usted ? "* You will also find the lower windows protected by iron *rejas*, through which, if you are on good terms with the black eyes within, you may perhaps kiss the tips of her tapering fingers.

There is a key to the heart of every Spaniard which has seldom failed me — the use of a little politeness. This always engages his attention. Add to it a dash of ceremony, and he is your friend at once. If you ask a Cuban for a light, he will first remove his hat, then his cigar, make you a low bow, and holding his fragrant Havana between his thumb and forefinger, with the lighted end towards himself, will present it to you with the air of a grandee that is at once graceful and captivating. If you follow his example and remain bareheaded until the courtesy is complete he will continue bowing until you are out of sight. If you are forgetful, and with thoughts intent upon your own affairs merely thank him and pass on, he will bless himself that he is not as other men

9

are, and dismiss you from his mind as one of those outside barbarians whom it is his duty to forget.

In Mexico the people are still more punctilious. To pass an acquaintance on the street without stopping, hat in hand, and inquiring one by one for his wife, children, and the various members of his household, and then waiting patiently until he goes through the same family list for you, is an unforgivable offence among friends. Even the native Indians are distinguished by an elaboration of manner in the courtesies they constantly extend to each other noted in no other serving people.

An old woman, barefooted, ragged, and dust-begrimed, leaning upon a staff, once preceded me up a narrow, crooked street. She looked like an animated fishnet hung on a fence to dry, so ragged and emaciated was she. A young Indian one half her age crossed her steps as she turned into a side street. Instantly he removed his hat and saluted her as if she had been the Queen of Sheba. *" A los pies de usted, señora "* (at your feet, lady), I heard him say as I passed. *" Bese usted las manos "* (my hands for your kisses, señor), replied she, with a bow which would have become a duchess.

I have lived long enough in Spanish countries

to adapt my own habits and regulate my own conduct to the requirements of these customs; and so when this morning in Guanajuato, I discovered that my only hope lay within the archway of the patio of this noble house, at once the residence of a man of wealth and of rank, I forthwith succumbed to the law of the country, with a result that doubly paid me for all the precious time it took to accomplish it; precious, because the whole front of the beautiful old church with its sloping flight of semicircular stone steps was now bathed in sunlight, and a few hours later the hot sun climbing to the zenith would round the corner of the tower, leave it in shadow, and so spoil its effect.

Within this door sat a fat, oily porter, rolling cigarettes. I approached him, handed him my card, and bade him convey it to his master together with my most distinguished considerations, and inform him that I was a painter from a distant city by the sea, and that I craved permission to erect my easel within the gates of his palace and from this coign of vantage paint the most sacred church across the way.

Before I had half examined the square of the patio, with its Moorish columns and arches and tropical garden filled with flowers, I heard quick footsteps above and caught sight of a group of gentlemen, preceded by an elderly man with bristling white hair, walking rapidly along the piazza of the second or living floor of the house.

In a moment more the whole party descended the marble staircase and approached me. The elderly man with the white hair held in his hand my card.

"With the greatest pleasure, señor," he said graciously. "You can use my doorway or any portion of my house; it is all yours; the view from the balcony above is much more extensive. Will you not ascend and see for yourself? But let me present you to my friends and insist that you first come to breakfast."

But I did not need the balcony, and it was impossible for me to share his coffee. The sun was moving, the day half gone, my stay in Guanajuato limited. If he would permit me to sit within the shadow of his gate I would ever bless his generosity, and, the sketch finished, would do myself the honor of appearing before him.

Half a dozen times during the progress of this picture the whole party ran down the staircase, napkins in hand, broke out into rapturous exclamations over its development, and insisted that some sort of nourishment, either solid or fluid, was absolutely necessary for the preserva-

tion of my life. Soon the populace began to
take an interest, and so blocked up the gateway that I could no longer follow the outlines
of the church. I remonstrated, and appealed
to my host. He grasped the situation, gave a
rapid order to the porter, who disappeared, and
almost immediately reappeared with an officer,
who saluted my host with marked respect. Five
minutes later a squad of soldiers cleared out
the archway and the street in front, formed
two files, and mounted guard until my work
was over. I began to wonder what manner of
man was this who gave away palaces and commanded armies!

At last the sketch was finished, and leaving
the porter in charge of my trap, I seized the
canvas, mounted the winding staircase, and
presented myself at the large door opening on
the balcony. At sight of me not only my host,
but all his guests, rose to their feet and welcomed me heartily, crowding about the chair
against which I propped the picture.

Then a door in the rear of the breakfast room
opened, and the señora and her two pretty
daughters glided in for a peep at the work of
the morning, declaring in one breath that it
was very wonderful that so many colors could
be put together in so short a time ; that I must

be *muy fatigado,* and that they would serve coffee for my refreshment at once.

This to a tramp, remember, discovered on a doorstep but a few hours before, with designs on the hallway !

This done I must see the garden and the parrots in the swinging cages and the miniature Chihuahua dogs, and last I must ascend the flight of brick steps leading to the roof and see the view from the tip-top of the house. It was when leaning over the projecting iron rail of this lookout, with the city below me and the range of hills above dotted with mining shafts, that I made bold to ask my host a direct question.

"Señor, it is easy for you to see what my life is and how I fill it. Tell me, what manner of man are you ? "

" *Con gusto, señor.* I am *un minero.* The shaft you see to the right is the entrance to my silver mine. I am *un agricultor.* I am *un agricultor.* Behind yon mountain lies my hacienda, and I am *un bienhechor* (a benefactor). The long white building you see to the left is the hospital which I built and gave to the poor of my town."

When I bade good-by to my miner, benefactor, and friend, I called a sad-faced Indian boy

14

who had watched me intently while at work, and who waited patiently until I reappeared. To him I consigned my " trap," with the exception of my umbrella staff, which serves me as a cane, and together we lost ourselves in the crowded thoroughfare.

"What is your name, *muchacho*?" I asked.

"Matías, señor."

"And what do you do?"

"Nothing."

"All day?"

"All day and all night, señor."

Here at least was a fellow Bohemian with whom I could loaf to my heart's content. I looked him over carefully. He had large dark eyes with drooping lids, which lent an air of extreme sadness to his handsome face. His curly black hair was crowded under his straw sombrero, with a few stray locks pushed through the crown. His shirt was open at the throat, and his leathern breeches, reaching to his knee, were held above his hips by a rag of a red sash edged with frayed silk fringe. Upon his feet were the sandals of the country. Whenever he spoke he touched his hat.

"And do you know Guanajuato?" I continued.

"Every stone, señor."

15

"Show it me."

In the old days this crooked old city of Guanajuato was known as *Quanashuato*, which in
the Tarascan tongue means the "Hill of the
Frogs;" not from the prevalence of that tooth-
some morsel, but because the Tarascan Indians,
according to Janvier, "found here a huge stone
in the shape of a frog, which they worshipped."
The city — at an elevation of 6800 feet — is
crowded into a narrow, deep ravine, terraced on
each side to give standing room for its houses.
The little Moorish-looking town of Marfil stands
guard at the entrance of the narrow gorge, its
heavy stone houses posted quite into the road,
and so blocking it up that the trains of mules
must needs dodge their way in and out to reach
the railroad below.

As you pass up the ravine you notice that
through its channel runs a sluggish, muddy
stream, into which is emptied all the filth of
the City of Frogs above, as well as all the
pumpings and waste washings of the silver
mines which line its sides below.

Into this mire droves of hogs wallow in the
hot sun, the mud caking to their sides and
backs. This, Matías tells me, their owners re-
ligiously wash off once a week to save the silver which it contains. As it is estimated that

the summer freshets have scoured from the bed
of this brook millions of dollars of silver since
the discovery of these mines in 1548, the owners cannot be blamed for scraping these beasts
clean, now that their output is reduced to a
mere bagatelle of six million dollars annually.

On you climb, looking down upon the houses
just passed on the street below, until you round
the great building of the Alhóndiga de Grana-
ditas, captured by the patriot priest Hidalgo in
1810, and still holding the iron spike which
spitted his head the year following. Then on
to the Plaza de Mejía Mora, a charming garden
park in the centre of the city.

This was my route, and here I sat down on
a stone bench surrounded by flowers, waving
palms, green grass, and pretty señoritas, and
listened to the music of a very creditable band
perched in a sort of Chinese pagoda in the park's
centre.

Matías was equal to the occasion. At my
request he ran to the corner and brought me
some oranges, a pot of coffee, and a roll, which
I shared with him on the marble slab, much to
the amusement of the bystanders, who could
not understand why I preferred lunching with
a street gamin on a park bench to dining with
the élite of Guanajuato at the café opposite.

The solution was easy. We were two tramps
with nothing to do.

Next Matías pointed out all the celebrities as
they strolled through the plaza, — the bishop
coming from mass, the governor and his secretary, and the beautiful Señorita Doña María,
who had been married the month before with
great pomp at the cathedral.

" And what church is that over the way
where I see the people kneeling outside,
Matías ?"

" The Iglesia de San Diego, señor. It is
Holy Thursday. To-day no one rides ; all the
horses are stabled. The señoritas walk to church
and wear black veils, and that is why so many
are in the streets. To-day and to-morrow the
mines are closed and all the miners are out in
the sunlight."

While Matías rattled on there swept by me
a cloud of lace encircling a bewitching face,
from out which snapped two wicked black eyes.
The Mexican beauties have more vivacity than
their cousins the Spaniards. It may be that the
Indian blood which runs in their veins gives
them a piquancy which reminds you more of
the sparkle of the French grisette than of the
languid air common to almost all high-bred
Spanish women.

18

She, too, twisted her pretty head, and a light laugh bubbled out from between her red lips and perfect teeth, as she caught sight of the unusual spectacle of a foreigner in knickerbockers breakfasting in the open air with a street tramp in sandals.

Seeing me divide an orange with Matías, she touched the arm of her companion, an elderly woman carrying a great fan, pointed me out, and then they both laughed immoderately. I arose gravely, and, removing my hat, saluted them with all the deference and respect I could concentrate into one prolonged curve of my spinal column. At this the duenna looked grave and half frightened, but the señorita returned to me only smiles, moved her fan gracefully, and entered the door of the church across the way.

" The caballero will *now* see the church ?" said the boy slowly, as if the incident ended the breakfast.

Later I did, and from behind a pillar, where I had hidden myself away from the sacristan, who frowned at my sketch-book, and where I could sketch and watch unobserved the penitents on their knees before the altar, I caught sight of my señorita snapping her eyes in the same mischievous way, and talking with her fan, as I have often seen the Spanish women do at the Tacon in Havana. It was not to me this time, but to a devout young fellow kneeling across the aisle. And so she prayed with her lips and talked with her heart and fan, and when it was all thus silently arranged between them, she bowed to the altar, and glided from the church without one glance at poor me, sketching behind the column. When I looked up again her lover had vanished.

Oh! the charm of this semi-tropical Spanish life! The balconies above the patios trellised with flowers; swinging hammocks; the slow plash of the fountains; the odor of jasmine wet with dew; the low thrum of guitar and click of castanet; the soft moonlight half revealing the muffled figures in lace and cloak! It is the same old story, and yet it seems to me it is told in Spanish lands more delightfully and with more romance, color, and mystery than elsewhere on the globe.

Matías woke me from my reverie.

" Señor, vespers in the cathedral at four."

So we wandered out into the sunlight, and joined the throng in holiday attire, drifting with the current towards the church of San Francisco. As we entered the side door to avoid the crowd, I stopped to examine a table piled high with rosaries and charms, presided over by a weather-beaten old woman, and covered with what was once an altar cloth of great beauty, embroidered in silver thread and silk. It was just faded and dingy enough to be harmonious, and just ragged enough to be interesting. In the bedecking of the sacred edifice for the festival days then approaching, the old wardrobes of the sacristy had been ransacked, and this piece, coming to light, had been thrown over the plain table as a background to the religious knickknacks.

Instantly a dozen schemes to possess it ran through my head. After all sorts of propositions, embracing another cloth, the price of two new ones, and a fresh table thrown in, I was confronted with this proposition : —

"You buy everything upon it, señor, and you can take the table and covering with you."

The service had already commenced. I could smell the burning incense, and hear the tinkling of the altar bell and the burst from the organ. The door by which we entered opened into a long passage running parallel with the church, and connecting with the sacristy, which ran immediately behind the altar. The dividing wall between this and the altar side of the church was a thin partition of wood, with grotesque openings near the ceiling. Through these the sounds of the service were so distinct that

every word could be understood. These openings proved to be between the backs of certain
saints and carvings, overlaid with gilt and forming the reredos.

Within the sacristy, and within five feet of
the bishop who was conducting the service, and
entirely undisturbed by our presence, sat four
hungry padres at a comfortable luncheon. Each
holy father had a bottle of red wine at his plate.
Every few minutes a priest would come in from
the church side of the partition, the sacristan
would remove his vestments, lay them away in
the wardrobes, and either robe him anew or hand
him his shovel hat and cane. During the process they all chatted together in the most unconcerned way possible, only lowering their voices
when the pauses in the service required it.

It may have been that the spiritual tasks of
the day were so prolonged and continuous that
there was no time for the material, and that it
was either here in the sacristy or go hungry.
Or perhaps it lifted for me one corner of the
sheet which covers the dead body of the religion of Mexico.

These corners, however, I will not uncover.
The sun shines for us all; the shadows are
cool and inviting; the flowers are free and
fragrant; the people courteous and hospitable

beyond belief ; the land the most picturesque and enchanting.

When I look into Matías's sad eyes and think to what a life of poverty and suffering he is doomed, and what his people have endured for ages, these ghosts of revolution, misrule, cruelty, superstition, and want rise up and confront me, and although I know that beneath this charm of atmosphere, color, and courtesy there lurks, like the deadly miasma of the ravine, lulled to sleep by the sunlight, much of degradation, injustice, and crime, still I will probe none of it. So I fill Matías's hand full of silver and copper coins, and his sad eyes full of joyful tears, and as I descend the rocky hill in the evening glow, and look up to the great prison of Guanajuato, with its roof fringed with rows of prisoners manacled together, and given this hour of fresh air because of the sacredness of the day, I forget their chains and the intrigue and treachery which forged many of them, and see only the purple city swimming in the golden light, and the deep shadows of the hills behind it.

II

AFTER DARK IN SILAO

CABALLERO! *A donde va usted?*"
"To Silao, to see the cathedral lighted."
"Alone?"

"*Cierto!* unless you go."

I was halfway across the open space dividing the railroad from the city of Silao when I was brought to a standstill by this inquiry. The questioner was my friend Morgan, an Englishman, who had lived ten years in the country and knew it thoroughly.

He was placed here in charge of the property of the road the day the last spike was driven, — a short, thickset, clear blue-eyed, and brown-bearded Briton, whose word was law, and whose brawny arm enforced it. He had a natural taste for my work, and we soon drifted together.

"Better take this," he continued, loosing his belt and handing me its contents, a row of cartridges and a revolver.

24

"Never carried one in my life."

"Well, you will now."

"Do you mean to say, Morgan, that I cannot cross this flat plain, hardly a quarter of a mile wide, and enter the city in safety without being armed?"

"I mean to say, *mi amigo*, that the mountains around Silao are infested with bandits, outlaws, and thieves; that these fellows prowl at night; that you are a stranger and recognized at sight as an American; that twenty-four hours after your arrival these facts were quietly whispered among the fraternity; that every article of value you have on down to your collar-button is already a subject of discussion and appraisement; that there are nine chances in ten that the blind cripple who sold you dulces this morning at the train was quietly making an inventory of your valuables, and that, had he been recognized by the guard, his legs would have untwisted themselves in a minute; that after dark in Silao is quite a different thing from under the gaslight in Broadway; and that unless you go armed you cannot go alone."

"But, Morgan, there is not a tree, stone, stump, or building in sight big enough to screen a rat behind. You can see even in the starlight

25

the entrance to the wide street leading to the cathedral.''

" Make no mistake, señor, these devils start up out of the ground. Strap this around you or stay here. Can you see my quarters — the small house near the Estacion ? Do you notice the portico with the sloping roof ? Well, my friend, I have sat on that portico in the cool of the evening and looked across this very plain and heard cries for help, and the next morning at dawn have seen the crowd gathered about a poor devil with a gash in his back the length of your hand.''

As we walked through the dust towards the city, Morgan continued : —

" The government are not altogether to blame for this state of things. They have done their best to break it up, and they have succeeded to a great extent. In Celaya alone the *jefe politico* showed me the records where he had shot one hundred and thirteen bandits in less than two years. He does not waste his time over judge or jury : strings them along in a row within an hour after they are caught plundering, then leaves them two days above ground as a warning to those who get away. Within a year to cross from Silao to Leon without a guard was as much as your life was worth. The diligence was robbed almost daily. This began to be a matter of course, and passengers reduced their luggage to the clothes they stood in. Finally the thieves confiscated these. Two years ago, old Don Palacio del Monte, whose hacienda is within five miles of here, started in a diligence one morning at daylight with his wife and two daughters and a young Mexican named Marquando, to attend a wedding feast at a neighboring plantation only a few miles distant. They were the only occupants. An hour after sunrise, while dragging up a steep hill, the coach came to a halt, the driver was pulled down and bound, old Palacio and Marquando covered with carbines, and every rag of clothing stripped from the entire party. Then they were politely informed by the chief, who was afterwards caught and shot, and who turned out to be the renegade son of the owner of the very hacienda where the wedding festivities were to be celebrated, to go home and inform their friends to bring more baggage in the future or some of them might catch cold !

"Marquando told me of it the week after it occurred. He was still suffering from the mortification. His description of the fat driver crawling up into his seat, and of the courteous old Mexican standing in the sunlight looking like a scourged mediæval saint, and of the dignified wave of his hand as he said to him, 'After you, señor,' before climbing up beside the driver, was delightful. I laughed over it for a week.''

'' What became of the señora and the girls ? '' I asked.

'' Oh, they slid in through the opposite door of the coach, and remained in seclusion until the driver reached an adobe hut and demanded of a peon family enough clothes to get the party into one of the outbuildings of the hacienda. There they were rescued by their friends.''

'' And Marquando ? '' I asked, — '' did he appear at the wedding ? ''

'' No. That was the hardest part of it. After the ladies were smuggled into the house, Don Palacio, by that time decorated with a straw mat and a sombrero, called Marquando aside. 'Señor,' he said with extreme gravity and deep pathos, ' after the events of the morning it will be impossible for us to recognize each other again. I entertain for you personally the most profound respect. Will you do me the great kindness of never speaking to me or any member of my family after to-day ? ' Marquando bowed and withdrew. A few months later he was in Leon. The governor gave a

ball. As he entered the room he caught sight of
Don Palacio surrounded by his wife and daughters. The old Mexican held up his hand, the
palm towards Marquando like a barrier. My
friend stopped, bowed to the floor, mounted his
horse, and left the city. It cut him deeply, too,
for he is a fine young fellow, and one of the
girls liked him.''

We had crossed the open space and were entering the city. Low buildings connected by
long .white adobe walls, against which grew
prickly pears, straggled out into the dusty plateau. Crooning over earthen pots balanced on
smouldering embers sat old hags, surrounded
by swarthy children watching the preparation
of their evening meal. Turning the sharp angle of the street, we stumbled over a group of
peons squatting on the sidewalk, their backs to
the wall, muffled to their eyes in their zarapes,
some asleep, others motionless, following us
with their eyes. Soon the spire of *la parróquia* loomed up in the starlight, its outlines
brought out into uncertain relief by the flickering light of the torches blazing in the market-
place below. Here Morgan stopped, and, pointing to a slit of an alley running between two
buildings and widening out into a square court,
said, —

"This is the entrance to an old patio long since abandoned. Some years ago a gang of cutthroats used it to hide their plunder. You can see how easy it would be for one of these devils to step behind you, put a stiletto between your shoulder blades, and bundle you in out of sight."

I crossed over and took the middle of the street. Morgan laughed.

"You are perfectly safe with me," he continued, "for I am known everywhere and would be missed. You might not. Then I adopt the custom of the country and carry an extra cartridge, and they know it. But you would be safe here anyway. It is only the outskirts of these Mexican towns that are dangerous to stroll around in after dark."

There is a law in Mexico called the *ley de fuego* — the law of fire. It is very easily understood. If a convict breaks away from the chain gang he takes his life in his hands. Instantly every carbine in the mounted guard is levelled, and a rattling fire is kept up until he either drops, riddled by balls, or escapes unhurt in the crevices of the foothills. Once away he is safe, and cannot be rearrested for the same crime. Silao has a number of these birds of freedom, and to their credit be it said, they are eminently respectable citizens. If he is overhauled by a ball, the pursuing squad detail a brace of convicts to dig a hole in the softest ground within reach, and a rude wooden cross the next day tells the whole story.

If a brigand has a misunderstanding with a citizen regarding the ownership of certain personal effects, the exclusive property of the citizen, and the brigand in the heat of the debate becomes careless in the use of his firearms, the same wooden cross announces the fact with an emphasis that is startling. Occurrences like these have been so frequent in the past that the country around Silao reminds one of an abandoned telegraph system, with nothing standing but the poles and cross-pieces.

Morgan imparted this last information from one of the stone seats in the alameda adjoining the church of Santiago, which we had reached and where we sat quietly smoking, surrounded by throngs of people pushing their way towards the open door of the sacred edifice. We threw away our cigarettes and followed the crowd.

It was the night of Good Friday, and the interior was ablaze with the light of thousands of wax candles suspended from the vaulted roof by fine wires, which swayed with the air from the great doors, while scattered through this

31

sprinkling of stars glistened sheets of gold-leaf strung on threads of silk. Ranged along the sides of the church upon a ledge just above the heads of the people sparkled a curious collection of cut-glass bottles, decanters, dishes, toilet-boxes, and goblets — in fact, every conceivable variety of domestic glass. Behind these in small oil-cups floated burned ends of candles and tapers. In the sacristy, upon a rude bier covered by an embroidered sheet, lay the wooden image of the dead Christ, surrounded by crowds of peons and Mexicans passing up to kiss the painted wounds and drop a few centavos for their sins and shortcomings.

As we passed out into the fresh night air, the glare of a torch fell upon an old man seated by a table, selling rosaries. Morgan leaned against one of the pillars of the railing surrounding the court, watched the traffic go on for a few minutes, and then, pointing to the entrance of the church, through which streamed the great flood of light, said, —

" Into that open door goes all the loose money of Mexico."

When we reached the plaza the people still thronged the streets. Venders sold dulces, fruits, candles, and the thousand and one knick-knacks bought in holiday times ; torches stuck

in the ground on high poles flared over the alameda ; groups of natives smoking cigarettes
chatted gayly near the fountain ; while lovers
in pairs disported themselves after the manner
of their kind under the trees. One young Indian girl and her dusky caballero greatly interested me. Nothing seemed to disturb them.
They cooed away in the full glare of a street
lantern as unconscious and unconcerned as if a
roof sheltered them. He had spread his blanket
so as to protect her from the cold stone bench.
It was not a very wide zarape, and yet there
was room enough for two.

The poverty of the pair was unmistakable.
A straw sombrero, cotton shirt, trousers, and
sandals completed his outfit; a chemise, blue
skirt, scarlet sash, and rebozo twisted about
her throat, her own. This humble raiment was
clean and fresh, and the red rose tucked coquet-
tishly among the braids of her purple-black
hair was just what was wanted to make it picturesque.

Both were smoking the same cigarette and
laughing between each puff, he protesting that
she should have two whiffs to his one, at which
there would be a little kittenish spatting, ending in his having his own way and kissing her
two cheeks for punishment.

With us, some love affairs end in smoke; here they seem to thrive upon it.

Morgan, however, did not seem to appreciate the love-making. He was impatient to return to the station, for it was nearly midnight.

"If you are going to supervise all the love affairs in Silao you might as well make a night of it," he laughed. So we turned from the plaza, entered a broad street, and followed along a high wall surrounding a large house, in reality the palace of Manuel Gonzalez, formerly President of the Republic. Here the crowds in the street began to thin out. By the time we reached another turn the city was deserted. Morgan struck a wax taper and consulted his watch.

"In ten minutes, *mi amigo*, the train is due from Chihuahua. I must be on hand to unlock the freight-house. We will make a short cut through here."

The moon had set, leaving to the flickering lanterns at the street corners the task of lighting us home. I stumbled along, keeping close to my friend, winding in and out of lonely, crooked streets, under black archways, and around the sharp projecting angles of low adobe walls. The only sound besides our hurrying foot-

34

steps was the loud crowing of a cock miscalcu-
lating the dawn.

Suddenly Morgan pushed aside a swinging
wooden door framed in an adobe wall, and I
followed him through what appeared to be an
abandoned convent garden. He halted on the
opposite side of the quadrangle, felt along the
whitewashed wall, shot back a bolt, and held
open a second door. As I closed it behind me a
man wrapped in a cloak stepped from a niche
in the wall and levelled his carbine. Morgan
sprang back and called out to me in a sharp, firm
voice, —

"Stand still."

I glued myself to the spot. In fact, the only
part of me that was at all alive was my imagi-
nation.

I was instantly perforated, stripped, and
lugged off to the mountains on a burro's back,
where select portions of my ears were sliced off
and forwarded to my friends as sight-drafts on
my entire worldly estate. While I was calculat-
ing the chances of my plunging through the
door and escaping by the garden, this came
from the muffled figure : —

" *Quien vive ?* "

" *La libertad,*" replied Morgan quietly.

35

" *Que nacion ?* "

" *Un compatriota,*" answered my companion.

The carbine was lowered slowly. Morgan advanced, mumbled a few words, called to me to follow, and struck out boldly across the plain to the station.

"Who was your murderous friend ? a brigand ?" I asked when I had recovered my breath.

"No; one of the Rurales, or civil guards. They are the salvation of the country. They challenge every man crossing their beat after ten o'clock."

"And if you do not halt — then what ?"

"Then say a short prayer. There will not be time for a long one."

As we reached the tracks I heard the whistle of the night express. Morgan seized a lantern and swung it above his head. The train stopped. I counted all my bones and turned in for the night.

III

THE OPALS OF QUERÉTARO

I ARRIVED with a cyclone. To be exact, the cyclone was ahead. All I saw as I stepped from the train was a whirling cloud of dust, through which the roof of the station was dimly outlined, a long plank walk, and a string of cabs.

A boy emerged from the cloud and grabbed my bag.

"Will it rain ?" I asked anxiously.

"No, señor. No rain, but much dust."

It was a dry storm, common in this season and section. Compared with it the simoon on the Sahara is a gentle zephyr.

When the boy had collected the balance of my belongings, he promptly asked me two questions. Would I visit the spot where Maximilian was shot, and would I buy some opals? The first was to be accomplished by means of a cab; the second by diving into his trousers pocket and hauling up a little wad. This he

37

unrolled, displaying half a teaspoonful of gems of more or less value and brilliancy.

I had not the slightest desire to see the spot, and my bank account was entirely too limited for opalescent luxuries. I imparted this information, rubbing both eyes and breathing through my sleeve. He could get me a cab and a hotel — anywhere out of this simoon.

" But, señor, it will be over in a minute."

Even while he spoke the sun sifted through, the blue sky appeared faintly overhead, and little whirls of funnel-shaped dust went careering down the track to plague the next town below.

When I reached the plaza the air was delicious and balmy, and the fountains under the trees cool and refreshing.

If one has absolutely nothing to do, Querétaro is the place in which to do it. If he suffers from the constitutional disease of being born tired, here is the place for him to rest. The grass grows in the middle of the streets; at every corner there is a small open square full of trees; under each tree a bench; on every bench a wayfarer: they are all resting. If you interview one of them as to his special occupation, he will revive long enough to search among the recesses of his wardrobe and fish out various

little wads. When he unwinds the skein of
dirty thread which binds one, he will spill out
upon his equally dirty palm a thimbleful of the
national gems, of more or less value.

You wonder where all these opalescent seed
pearls come from, and conclude that each one of
these weary dealers has an especial hole in the
ground somewhere which he visits at night.
Hence his wads, his weariness, and his daytime
loaf.

In reply to your inquiries he says, in a vague
sort of a way, "Oh! from the mines;" but
whether they are across the mountains or in
his back yard you never know. Of one thing
you are convinced: to be retailed by the wad,
these gems must be wholesaled by the bushel.
You can hardly jostle a man in Querétaro who
has not a collection somewhere about him. The
flower-woman at the corner, the water-carrier
with his red jars, the cabby, the express agent,
the policeman, and I doubt not the padre and
the sacristan, all have their little wads tucked
away somewhere in their little pockets.

And yet with all this no one ever saw, within
the memory of the oldest inhabitant, a single
stone in the ear or on the finger of any citizen of Querétaro. They are hoarded for the
especial benefit of the stranger. If he is a poor

stranger and has but one peseta, it makes no difference, he must have an opal, and the spoonful is raked over until a little one for a peseta is found. Quite an electric light of a gem can be purchased for five dollars.

The spot and the opal are, however, the only drawbacks to the stranger, and even then, if it becomes known that upon no possible condition could you be induced to climb that forlorn hill, halfway up which the poor emperor was riddled to death, and that you have been born not only tired but with the superstition that opals are unlucky, then by a kind of freemasonry the word is passed around, and you are spared, and welcomed. This was my experience. The well-known poverty of the painter the world over — instantly recognized when I opened my umbrella — assisted me, no doubt, in establishing this relation.

But the charm of Querétaro is not confined to its grass-grown streets. The churches are especially interesting. That of Santa Cruz is entirely unique, particularly its interior adornment. Besides, there is a great aqueduct, five miles long, built on stone arches, — the most important work of its kind in Mexico, — supplying fresh, cool water from the mountains, the greatest of all blessings in a thirsty land. Then there are scores of fountains scattered through the city, semi-tropical plants in the plazas, palms and bananas over the walks, and on the edge of the city a delightful alameda, filled with trees and embowered in roses. The flowers are free to whoever will gather. Moreover, on the corners of the streets, under the arching palms, sit Indian women selling water from great red earthen jars.

With that delicate, refined taste which characterizes these people in everything they touch, the rims of these jars are wreathed with poppies, while over their sides hang festoons of leaves. The whole has a refreshing look which must be enjoyed to be appreciated. I put down half a centavo, the smallest of copper coins, and up came a glass of almost ice-cold water from the jars of soft-baked porous clay.

Then there is the church of Santa Clara, a smoky, dingy old church, with sunken floors and a generally dilapidated appearance within — until you begin to analyze its details. Imagine a door leading from the main body of the church — it is not large — to the sacristy. The door proper is the inside beading of an old picture frame. Across the top is a heavy silk curtain of faded pomegranate. Around the beading extend the several members of a larger and still larger frame, in grooves, flutes, scrolls, and rich elaborate carving clear to the ceiling, the whole forming one enormous frame of solid gilt. In and out of this yellow gold door little black dots of priests and penitents sway the pomegranate curtain, looped back to let them pass. To the right rises a high choir loft overlaid with gold-leaf. Scattered about on the walls, unplaced, as it were, hang old pictures and tattered banners. On the left stands the altar, raised above the level of the church, surrounded by threadbare velvet chairs, and high candelabra resting on the floor, holding giant candles. Above these hang dingy old lamps of exquisite design. The light struggles through the windows, begrimed with dust. The uncertain benches are polished smooth. At the far end a sort of partition of open wooden slats shuts off the altar rail. Behind this screen is stored a lumber of old furniture, great chests, wooden images, and the abandoned and worn-out paraphernalia of religious festivals.

Yet with all this Santa Clara is the most delightfully picturesque church interior one can meet with, the world over. Some day they will take up a collection, or an old Don will die and leave a pot of money " to restore and beautify the most holy and sacred church of Santa Clara," and the fiends will enter in and close the church, and pull down the old pictures and throw away the lamps, chairs, and candlesticks, and white-wash the walls, regild the huge frame of the sacristy door, and make dust-rags of the pome-granate silk. Then they will hang a green and purple raw silk terror, bordered with silver braid, in its place, panel the whitewashed walls in red stripes, bracket pressed-glass kero-sene lamps on the columns, open the edifice to the public, and sing Te Deums for a month, in honor of the donor.

This is not an exaggeration. Step into the church of San Francisco, now the cathedral of Querétaro, within half a dozen squares of this lovely old church of Santa Clara, and see the ruin that has been wrought. I forget the name of the distinguished old devotee who contributed his estate to destroy this once beautiful church, but his soul ought to do penance in purgatory until the fingers of time shall have regilded its interior with the soft bloom of the dust and mould of centuries, and the light of countless summers shall have faded into pale harmonies the impious contrasts he left behind him.

I often think what a shock it must be to the good taste of nature when one whitewashes an old fence. For years the sun bleached it, and the winds polished it until each fibre shone like soft threads of gray satin. Then the little lichens went to work and filled up all the cracks and crannies, and wove gray and black films of lace over the rails, and the dew came every night and helped the green moss to bind the edges with velvet, and the worms gnawed the splinters into holes, and the weeds clustered about it and threw their tall blossoms against it, and where there was found the top of a particularly ugly old hewn post a little creeper of a vine peeped over the stone wall and saw its chance and called out, "Hold on; I can hide that," and so shot out a long, delicate spray of green, which clung faithfully all summer and left a crown of gold behind when it died in the autumn. And yet here comes this vandal with a scythe and a bucket, sweeps away all this beauty in an hour, and leaves behind only its grinning skeleton.

A man who could whitewash an old worm fence would be guilty of any crime, — even of boiling a peach.

But with the exception of the cathedral, this imp of a bucket has fastened very little of his fatal work upon Querétaro.

When the sun goes down behind the trees of the plaza the closely barred shutters, closed

44

all day, are bowed open, and between the slats you can catch the flash of a pair of dark eyes. Later, the fair owners come out on the balconies one by one, their dark hair so elaborately wrought that you know at a glance how the greater part of the afternoon has been spent. When the twilight steals on, the doors of these lonely and apparently uninhabited houses are thrown wide open, displaying the exquisite gardens blooming in the patios, and through the gratings of the always closed iron gates you get glimpses of easy-chairs and hammocks with indented pillows, telling the story of the day's exertion. In the twilight you pass these same pretty señoritas, in groups of threes and fours, strolling through the parks, dressed in pink and white lawn, with Spanish veils and fans, their dainty feet clad in white stockings and red-heeled slippers.

One makes friends easily among a people so isolated. When it is once understood that although an American you are not connected with the railway, their hospitality is most cordial.

"I like you," said an old man seated next me on a bench in the plaza one afternoon, "because you are an American and do not eat the tobacco. *Caramba!* that is horrible!"

My trap, moreover, is a constant source of

astonishment and amusement. No sooner is the umbrella raised and I get fairly to work than I am surrounded by a crowd so dense I cannot see a rod ahead. It is so rare that a painter is seen in the streets — many people tell me that they never saw one at work before — that often I rise from my stool in despair at the backs and shoulders in front. I then pick out some one or two having authority, and stand them guard over each wing of the half circle, and so the sketch is completed.

This old fellow who shared my bench in the plaza had served me in this capacity in the morning, and our acquaintance soon ripened into an intimacy. He was a clean, cool, breezy-looking old fellow, with a wide straw sombrero shading a ruddy face framed in a bushy, snow-white beard. His coat, trousers, shirt, and sandals were all apparently cut from the same piece of white cotton cloth. The only bit of color about him below his rosy face was a zarape. This, from successive washings, — an unusual treatment, by the way, for zarapes, — had faded to a delicate pink.

"Not made now," said he, in answer to my inquiring glance. "This zarape belonged to my father, and was woven by my grandmother on a hand loom. You can get plenty at the store.

They are made by steam, but I cannot part with this. It is for my son.''

I reluctantly gave it up. It was the best I had seen. When he stood up and wrapped it about him he was as delicious a bit of color as one would find in a day's journey. Moreover, the old fellow was a man of information. He knew the history of the founding of the city and the building of the great aqueduct by the Marques de la Villa del Villar de la Aguila, who defrayed most of the expenses, and whose effigy decorates the principal fountain. He saw Maximilian and Generals Miramon and Mejía leave the convent of Santa Cruz the morning of their execution, June 19, 1867; and remembered perfectly the war with the United States and the day the treaty of peace was ratified with Congress in 1848. Finally he tells me that pulque was first discovered in Querétaro, and insists that, as this is my last day in the city, — for on the morrow I go to Aguas Calientes, — I must go to the posada opposite and have a mug with him; that when I reach the great city of Mexico I will think of this pulque, the most delicious in the republic, and finding none to compare, will come back to Querétaro for its mate, and so he will see me again.

We have the pulque, the old man drinking

my share, and on our way to the station pass through the market-place. My last view of this delightful old city is across this market-place, with the domed buildings in the background silhouetted against the evening sky. All over the open space where the rush and traffic of the morning had held sway now lounged and slept hundreds of tired people, some on the steps surrounding the square stone column centring the plaza, others flat on the pavement. Here they will doze until the sun looks at them from over the Cerro de las Campañas. Then they will shake themselves together, and each one will go in search of his daily avocation. It is safe to say that not one in ten ever finds it.

IV

SOME PEONS AT AGUAS CALIENTES

BLINDING sunlight; a broad road ankle deep in dust; a double row of great trees with branches like twisted cobras; inky blue-black shadows stencilled on the gray dust, repeating the tree forms above; a long, narrow canal, but a few feet wide, half filled with water, from which rise little whiffs of hot steam; beside it a straggling rude stone wall fringed with bushes. In the middle distance, through vistas of tree trunks, glimpses of brown fields fading away into pale pink, violet, and green. In the dim blue beyond, the dome and towers of a church, surmounting little spots of yellow, cream white, and red, broken with patches of dark green, — locating bits of the town, — with orange groves between.

Long strings of burros crawl into the city along this highway, loaded down with great bundles of green fodder; undulating masses of yellow dust drift over it, which harden into droves of sheep as they pass.

49

Shuffling along its edges, hugging the intermittent shadows, stroll groups of natives in
twos and threes ; the women in straw hats with
plaited hair, their little children slung to their
backs, the men in zarapes and sandals, carrying
crates on their shoulders packed with live poul-
try and cheap pottery.

Such was my first glance at Aguas Calientes.
But there is something more. To the left, along
the whole length of the canal or sluiceway, as
far as the eye can reach, are scattered hundreds of
natives of both sexes, and all ages, lining the
water's edge and disporting themselves in every
conceivable state of *déshabille*. In fact, it might
as well be stated that the assemblage is divided
into two classes, those who have something on
and those who have nothing. Five hundred of
the descendants of Montezuma quietly taking
their baths at high noon on a public highway,
with only such privacy as the Republic of Mexico and the blue sky of heaven afford !

Old men hobble along the roadside, turn off
to the left, select a convenient bush as a clothes-
rack, scale off what scanty raiment they carry
with them, and slide turtle-like into the warm
water. Young Indian girls in bunches of half a
dozen sit by the canal and comb out their wavy
black hair, glossy with wet, while they chat

50

merrily with their friends, whose heads bob up over the brink, and whose bodies simmer at a temperature of 90°. Whole families soak in groups, sousing their babies in the warm water and draining them on the bank, where they glisten in the dazzling sunlight like bronzed Cupids. Now and then a tall, straight young Indian turns aside from out the dust, winds his zarape about him, and protected by its folds unmakes his toilet, and disappears over the edge.

Up and down this curious inland Long Branch rows of heads bob up from the sluiceway and smile good-naturedly as I draw near. They are not abashed or disturbed in the slightest degree ; they are only concerned lest I seek to crowd them from their places, theirs by right of oc- cupancy.

Even the young women lying on the bank in the shade, with one end of a zarape tossed over their backs, their only other garment washed and drying in the sun, seem more interested in the sketch trap than in him who carries it. It is one of the customs of the country.

It is true that near the springs above, within a mile of this spot, there is a small pond filled from the overflow of the baths adjoining, which they can use and sometimes do, but the privacy is none the greater. It is equally true that down the road nearer the city there are also the "Baños Grandes," where for one peseta — about twenty-five cents — they can obtain a bath with all the encircling privacy of stone walls, and with the additional comforts of a crash towel, one foot square, and a cake of soap of the size and density of a grapeshot. But then, the wages of a native for a whole day's work is less than one peseta, and when he is lucky enough to get this, every centavo in it is needed for the inside of his dust-covered body.

Nor can he utilize his surplus clothing as a shield and cover. He has but one suit, a white shirt and a pair of cotton trousers. Naturally he falls back upon his zarape, often handling it as skilfully and effectively as the Indian women on the steps leading to the sacred Ganges do their gorgeous colored tunics, slipping the dry one over the wet without much more than a glimpse of finger and toe.

All these thoughts ran through my head as I unlimbered my trap, opened my white umbrella, and put up my easel to paint the curious scene.

"*Buenos dias, señor,*" came a voice over my shoulder. I looked up and into the dark eyes of a swarthy Mexican, who was regarding me with

52

much the same air as one would a street ped-
dler preparing to exhibit his wares.

"Does everybody hereabout bathe in the
open air ? " I ventured to ask.

"Why not ? It is either here or not at all,"
he replied.

I continued at work, ruminating over the
strange surroundings, the query unanswered.

Why not, in fact ? A tropical sun, clouds of
dust dry as powder and fine as smoke, air and
water free, — nothing else in their life of slavery.

One has only to look into these sad faces to
read the history of this patient, uncomplaining
race, or to watch them as they sit for hours
in the shadow of some great building, motionless, muffled to the mouth in their zarapes and
rebozos, their eyes looking straight ahead as if
determined to read the future, — to appreciate
their helplessness.

From the days of Cortez down to the time
of Diaz, they have been humiliated, degraded,
and enslaved ; all their patriotism, self-reliance,
and independence have long since been crushed
out. They are a serving people, set apart and
kept apart by a *caste* as defined and rigid as
divides society to-day in Hindoostan — infinitely more severe than ever existed in the

most benighted section of our own country in the old plantation days.

They have inherited nothing in the past but poverty and suffering, and expect nothing in the future. To sleep, to awake, to be hungry, to sleep again. Sheltered by adobe huts, sleeping upon coarse straw mats, their only utensils the rude earthen vessels they make themselves, their daily food but bruised corn pounded in a stone mortar, they pass their lives awaiting the inevitable, without hope and without ambition.

" As a rule," says Consul-General Strother (Porte Crayon), "none of the working classes of Mexico have any idea of present economy or of providing for the future. The lives of most of them seem to be occupied in obtaining food and amusement for the passing hour, without either hope or desire for a better future."

David A. Wells, in his terse and pithy " Study of Mexico," speaking of the haciendas, and their peon labor, says : —

" The owners of these large Mexican estates, who are generally men of wealth and education, rarely live upon them, but make their homes in the city of Mexico or in Europe, and intrust the management of their property to a superintendent, who, like the owner, considers himself a gentleman, and whose chief business

54

is to keep the peons in debt, or, what is the same thing, in slavery. Whatever work is done is performed by the peons, — in whose veins Indian blood predominates, — in their own way and in their own time. . . . Without being bred to any mechanical profession, the peons make and repair nearly every instrument or tool that is used upon the estate, and this, too, without the use of a forge, not even of bolts and nails. The explanation of such an apparently marvellous result is to be found in a single word, or rather material, rawhide, — with which the peon feels himself qualified to meet almost any constructive emergency, from the framing of a house to the making of a loom, the mending of a gun, or the repair of a broken leg.''

It is not, therefore, from lack of intelligence, or ingenuity, or capacity, that the condition of these descendants of the Aztec warriors is so hopeless, but rather from the social isolation to which they are subjected, and which cuts them off from every influence that makes the white man their superior.

So I worked on, pondering over this hopeless race, outcasts and serfs in a land once their own, and thinking of the long account of cruelty and selfishness which stood against the Spanish nation, when suddenly from beneath my white umbrella I noticed three Indians rise from the ground near the canal, stand apart from their fellows, and walk towards me. As I lifted my eyes they hesitated, then, as if gathering courage, again advanced cautiously until they stood within a dozen yards of my easel. Here they squatted in the dust, the three in a row, their zarapes half covering their faces. I laid down my palette and beckoned them to me. They advanced smiling, raised their sombreros with an " *A Dios, señor,*" crouched down on their haunches, a favorite attitude, and watched every movement of my brush with the deepest interest, exchanging significant and appreciative glances as I dotted in the figures. Not one opened his lips. Silent and grave as the stone gods of their ancestors sat they, wholly absorbed in a revelation as astounding to them as a vision from an unknown world.

Presently a great flock of sheep wrinkled past me, shutting out my view, and I reversed my canvas to shield it, and waited for the dust to settle. During the pause I slipped my hand into the side pocket of my blouse, drew out my cigarette case, and, touching the spring, handed its open contents to the three Indians.

It was curious to see how they received the

slight courtesy, and with what surprise, hesi-
tancy, and genuine delight they looked at the
open case. It was as if you had stopped a crip-
pled beggar on the road, and, having relieved
his wants, had lifted him up beside you and
returned him to his hovel in your carriage.

Each man helped himself daintily to my cigarettes, laying them on the palm of his hand, and
then watched me closely. I selected my own,
touched my match-safe, and passed the lighted
taper to the Indian nearest me. Instantly they
all uncovered, placing their sombreros in the
dust, and gravely accepted the light. When I
had exhausted its flickering flame upon my own
cigarette, and taken my first whiff, they replaced their hats with the same sort of respectful silence one sometimes sees in a crowded
street when a priestly procession passes. It was
not a matter of form alone. It did not seem to
be simply the acknowledgment of perhaps the
most trivial courtesy one can offer another in a
Spanish country. There was something more
that lurked around the corners of their mouths
and kindled in their eyes, which said to me but
too plainly, —

"This stranger is a white man, and yet he
does not despise us."

When the sketch was finished, the trap

57

packed, and I turned to retrace my steps to my lodgings, all three arose to their feet, unwound their zarapes, and trailed them in the dust. I can see them now, standing uncovered in the sunlight, and hear their low, soft voices calling after me, —

"*Con Dios va usted, mi amigo.*"

I continued my rambles, following the highway into the city, idling about the streets, and jotting down queer bits of architecture and odd figures in my sketch-book. I stopped long enough to examine the high saddles of a pair of horses tethered outside a *fonda*, their owners drinking pulque within, and then crossed over to where some children were playing "bull-fight."

When the sun went down I strolled into the beautiful garden of San Marcos and sat me down on one of the stone benches surrounding the fountain. Here, after bathing my face and hands in the cool water of the basin, I rested and talked to the gardener.

He was an Indian, quite an old man, and had spent most of his life here. The garden belonged to the city, and he was paid two pesetas a day to take care of his part of it. If I would come in the evening the benches would be full.

There were many beautiful señoritas in Aguas
Calientes, and on Sunday there would be music. But I must wait until April if I wanted to
see the garden, and in fact the whole city in its
gala dress. Then would be celebrated the *fiesta*
of San Marcos, their patron saint, strings of
lanterns hung and lighted, the fountains playing, music everywhere, and crowds of people
from all the country around, even from the
great city of Mexico, and as far north as Zacatécas. Then he tucked a cluster of azaleas into
the strap of my " trap " and insisted on going
with me to the corner of the cathedral, so that
I should not miss the turn in the next street
that led to the pottery market.

All the markets of Aguas Calientes are interesting, for the country round about is singularly rich and fertile, and fruits and vegetables
are raised in abundance. The pottery market is
especially so. It is held in a small open square
near the general market, surrounded by high
buildings. The pottery is piled in great heaps
on the ground, and the Indian women, sheltered by huge square and octagon umbrellas of
coarse matting, sit all day serving their cus-
tomers. At night they burn torches. All the
other markets are closed at noon. The pottery
is very cheap, a few centavos covering the cost

of almost any single piece of moderate size, and one peseta making you master of the most important specimen in a collection.

Each province, in fact almost every village in Mexico, produces a ware having more or less distinctly marked characteristics. In Guadalajara the pottery is gray, soft-baked, and unglazed, but highly polished and often decorated with stripings of silver and gold bronze. In Zacatécas the glaze is as hard and brilliant as a piano top, and the small pulque pots and pitchers look like polished mahogany or highly colored meerschaum pipe bowls. In Puebla a finer ware is made, something between good earthenware and coarse, soft porcelain. It has a thick tin glaze, and the decoration in strong color is an under-glaze. Here in Aguas Calientes they make not only most of these coarser varieties, but a better grade of gray stoneware, covered with a yellow glaze, semi-transparent, with splashings of red flowers and leaves scattered over it.

The potters are these much despised, degraded peons, who not only work in clay, embroider in feathers with exquisite results (an industry of their ancestors), but make the finer saddles of stamped and incised leather, besides producing an infinite variety of horse equipment unknown outside of Mexico. Moreover, in Uruápam they make Japanese lacquers, in Santa Fé on Lake Pátzcuaro, Moorish iridescent ware, and near Puebla, Venetian glass. In a small town in western Mexico I found a glass pitcher, made by a Tarascan Indian, of such exquisite mould and finish that one unfamiliar with the handiwork of this down-trodden race, seeing it in its place of honor in my studio, would say, " Ah, Venetian ! Salviati, of course."

From the market I sought the church of San Diego, with its inlaid wooden floor and quaint doorway richly carved, and as the twilight settled, entered the narrow street that led to my lodgings. At the farther end, beneath an overhanging balcony, a group of children and natives were gathered about a band of wandering minstrels. As I drew near, the tinkle of a triangle and the thrum of a harp accompanying a weird chant rose on the air. The quartette in appearance, costume, and bearing were quite different from any of the Indians I had seen about Aguas Calientes. They were much lighter in color, and were distinguished by a certain air of independence and dignity.

The tallest and oldest of the band held in his left hand a short harp, quite Greek in its design. The youngest shook a tambourine, with rim and rattles complete, but without the drum-head. The third tinkled a triangle, while the fourth, a delicate-looking, large-eyed, straight young fellow, handsome as a Greek god, with teeth like rows of corn, joined in the rhythmic chant. As they stood in the darkening shadows, beating time with their sandalled feet, with harp and triangle silhouetted against the even-ing sky, and zarapes hanging in long straight lines from their shoulders, the effect was so thoroughly classic that I could not but recall one of the great friezes of the Parthenon. I lighted a cigarette, opened the window of my balcony, and placing the bits of pottery I had bought in the market in a row on my window-sill, with the old gardener's azaleas in the largest jar, listened to the music, my thoughts full of the day's work and experience. My memory went back to my three friends of the morning, standing in the sunlight, their sombreros in the dust ; to the garrulous old gardener bending over his flowers ; to the girl selling pottery ; to the almost tender courtesy and gentleness of these people, their unchanging serenity of tem-per, their marvellous patience, their innate taste and skill, their hopeless poverty and daily pri-

vations and sufferings; and finally to the injustice of it all.

Peons and serfs in their own land ! Despoiled
by Cortez, tricked by his successors, enslaved
by the viceroys, taxed, beaten, defrauded, and
despised by almost every ruler and usurper
since the days of Spanish rule, the whole history of the life of the Aztec and his descendants,
from the initial massacre at Cholula down to the
present day, has been one long list of cruelty
and deceit.

The music ceased. The old minstrel approached the balcony and held up his wide sombrero. I poured into it all my stock of copper
coin. " *Muchas gracias, señor,*" came back the
humble acknowledgment. Then they disappeared up the narrow street and the crowd dispersed. I looked after them long and musingly,
and surprised myself repeating the benediction
of the morning : —

" *Con Dios vayan ustedes, mis amigos.*"

V

THE OLD CHAIR IN THE SACRISTY
AT ZACATÉCAS.

IT stood just inside the door as I entered from
the main body of the church. Richly carved,
with great arms broadened out where the elbows touched, it had the air of being especially
designed for some overfed, lazy prelate. The
hand-rests were rounded in wide flutes, convenient spaces for his fat fingers. The legs bowed
out slightly from the seat, then curved sharply,
and finally terminated in four grotesque claws,
each clutching a great round ball, — here his
toes rested. The back and seat were covered
with the rags and remnants of a once rich velvet, fastened by an intermittent row of brass
nails, some headless, and others showing only
the indent of their former usefulness. On each
corner of the back flared two gilt flambeaux,
standing bolt upright like a pair of outspread
hands. Over the whole was sifted, and into
each crack, split, and carving was grimed and

64

channelled, the white dust that envelops Zacatécas like an atmosphere.

The old chair had evidently had its day, and
it had been a glorious one. What ceremonies,
what processions, masses, feasts, had it presided over! What grave counsels had it listened to! What dangers escaped, the last but
a score of years ago, when this same old cathedral of Nuestra Señora de la Asuncion was bom-
barded by Juarez!

Its curved and stately lines were too graceful
for Mexican handiwork. Perhaps some old Spanish grandee, with penitence in his soul, had sent
this noble seat across the sea to the new Spain,
in grateful remembrance of the most holy and
blessed Lady of Guadaloupe, the patron saint
of this once powerful church.

If, in the old days, it had belonged to a set
of twelve, or, by reason of its arms, had presided over a family less blessed, no fragment of
back, leg, or round was left to tell the tale. A
plain square table, covered with a cotton cloth
edged with cheap lace, upon which stood a
crucifix, a few worn-out, high-backed, hide-
bottomed chairs, and a chest of green painted
bureau drawers built into the wall and holding
the church vestments, were its only companions.
But all these were of a recent date and pattern.

65

I had been in Zacatécas but a few hours when I discovered this precious relic of the last century. I coveted it at sight, — more, I admit, than I dared tell the good-natured, patient sacristan who stood by wondering and delighted, watching me make a rapid sketch of its twisted legs and capacious seat. To all my propositions for its immediate possession, however, he only shrugged his shoulders. I confess that many of them savored of conspiracy, and all of them of grand larceny, and that I was entitled to a speedy trial and a place in the chain-gang for suggesting any one of them.

" A ragged old chair that will hardly stand upright; the only one left. Who will miss it ?" I argued.

"The padre, señor painter, who is very old. He loves everything here. This wretched chair has been his friend for many years."

"Tell him, *mi amigo*, that I, too, love chairs, and old ones especially, and will give him the price of two, four, six new ones for this old rattletrap."

"Very well, señor ; at five o'clock to-day vespers will be over. Then the padre will return here. Wait for me in the garden over the way near the fountain."

The decision was a relief. In Mexico, as in

66

Spain, it is generally to-morrow or the day after. *Mañana por la mañana* is the motto of the Spanish-speaking race.

It was now twelve o'clock. Only five hours to wait. My hopes rose. I reëntered the cathedral.

It had been a sumptuous church in its day. Begun in 1612, completed one hundred and twenty-five years later, and dedicated with imposing ceremonies the year following, it had contained within its walls all that florid magnificence which distinguishes the Mexican churches. All the interior adornments had been of plated gilt, the altars of fine marble and onyx, the font of solid silver, — alone valued at twenty thousand pounds sterling. Four noble steps of colored marble, still intact, led the way to the altar. On each side ran a railing of wrought silver of fabulous worth. Over this had hung a lamp of splendid proportions, burning a single taper, and shedding a ruby light. The main floor was of marquetry of varied colored woods, and of a simple Moorish pattern, marking the prominence of that Spanish taste which at the period characterized so many of the great colonial structures.

But sad changes had taken place since that date, most of them within the last quarter of

this century. Not only had the superb silver
altar-rail, hanging lamp, and costly font been
coined down into Mexican dollars, but tapestries
and velvets, chasubles and copes, heavy with
embroidery in gold and silver, had also found
their way to the crucible. Even the intricate
marquetry floor had been broken up, presumably in the search for hidden vessels, and in its
place here and there were great squares of
heavy planking held down by rude iron spikes,
the heads thrust up and kept bright by the restless feet of countless worshippers.

The leaders of an impecunious government
executing a forced loan do not stop at trifles like
these !

As I wandered about, comparing its present
shabby surroundings with the record of its past
grandeur, groups of penitents would glide in,
throw their rebozos from their faces, and kneel
praying. Near me a single figure closely muffled would press her face against the sliding panel
of the queer confessional box and pour into the
ear of the listless priest the story of her sin.
Over by the altar a solitary Indian, wrapped in
his zarape, his wide straw sombrero by his side,
would bend forward until his forehead touched
the cold pavement and so remain motionless.
About in the aisles or prostrate before the rude

wooden figures of the saints knelt other groups of worshippers, often an entire family together, telling their beads with their lips and watching me with their eyes as I noted in my sketch-book the picturesque bits about me. Finally I completed the circuit of the interior, and a flood of sunlight poured in through an open door. This led me to the street and so on into the market-place.

No such scene exists in any quarter of the globe where I have wandered : a brilliant sky blue as a china plate ; blinding sunlight ; throngs of people in red, orange, or blue ; women in re-bozos and scarlet sashes ; men wearing vermil-ion zarapes about their shoulders, with wide hats of felt trimmed with silver, and breeches of pink buckskin held together down the sides by silver buttons ; donkeys piled high with great sacks of silver ore ; cavaliers on horse-back with murderous rowels in the heels of their riding-boots, their Mexican saddles fes-tooned with lassos and lariats ; soldiers carry-ing carbines and mounted on spirited horses guarding gangs of convicts, each one of whom staggers under a basket of sand held to his back by a strap across his forehead ; great flocks of sheep blocking up the narrow streets, driven by shepherds on horseback, changing their pasture from one hillside to another, — the whole completes a picture as strange as it is unique.

In the centre of the plaza stands a curious fountain, surrounded by a low wall breast-high. Around this swarm hundreds of women. Hanging over it are half a hundred more, reaching as far across the circular wall as their arms will permit, scooping up the thin sheet of water into saucers with which they filled their jars. On the pavement, protected by huge square umbrellas of straw mats, with ribs like a boy's kite, squatting Indian women sell oranges, prickly pears, figs, lemons, *cherimoyis*, great melons, and other tropical fruits. On the corners of the streets, under rags of awning, sit cobblers ready to cut and fit a sandal while you wait, their whole stock in trade but a pile of scraps of sole leather, a trifle larger than the human foot, some leather thongs, and a sharp curved knife. Adjoining the market, facing an open square, rises a great building supported by immense square pillars forming an arcade. At the foot of each pillar a garrulous Mexican shouts out the wares of his impromptu shop at half-minute intervals. Then comes the alameda, or public garden, bright with flowers and semi-tropical plants, with a summer-house of the time-honored pattern, octagon, lined with benches,

70

and in the centre a table containing, as usual, the fragments of the last lounger's lunch.

Here I rested out of the glare and din.

Suddenly, while looking down upon the street across the green, listening to the plash of the fountain and watching the señoritas on their way to mass, I saw a rush of people crowding the streets below, and heard the clear musical notes of a woman's voice rising above the street cries. As the mob forced its way past the corner leading from the cathedral and up the main street fronting me, I caught sight of a ceremony not often seen in Zacatécas, and but rarely met with elsewhere.

In the middle of the street, upon their knees on the rough stones, walked or rather crawled two native Indian girls dressed in white, their heads bare, their black hair streaming down their backs, their eyes aflame with excitement. Both clasped to their breasts a small crucifix. Surrounding them were a dozen half-crazed devotees, whose frenzied cries swelled the chant of the youngest penitent. Suddenly, from out a pulque shop on the opposite corner, darted three men, evidently peons. With a quick movement they divided the pressing crowd, sprang ahead of the girls, and tearing their own zarapes from their shoulders, threw them in turn in front of the penitents. As the girls crawled across them, the first peon would again seize his zarape, run ahead, and respread it.

"It is a penance, señor," said a bystander, evidently a Spaniard, "not often seen here. The girls believe they have committed some great sin. They are on their way to Los Reme-dios, the chapel that you see on the hill yonder. But for these drunken peons they would leave a bloody track."

Whether drunk or sober, by bigot or scoffer, it was a graceful act. Surely the gallant Sir Walter paid no more courtly tribute to the good Queen Bess when he threw his cloak beneath her dainty feet than did these poor peons to their dusky sisters.

But it was still some hours before the padre would be at leisure and I get definite news of my coveted chair.

I would lunch at the Zacatecano, formerly the old Augustinian convent, now the only inn this quaint old town can boast of, take a run by the tram to Guadaloupe, past the silver mines, and be back in time for the sacristan.

As I entered, the landlord extended both hands as if he had been my dearest friend. He proved to be, later.

"Certainly, señor. What shall it be? We

72

have a cutlet ; we also have a salad. Beer ? Plenty. San Louis, Bass, Mexican. Which shall I open for the illustrious painter ?''

The painter ordered a bottle of Bass, and being thirsty and a long way from home, and with the remembrance of many a foaming tankard in other benighted quarters of the earth, ordered another. If the landlord was polite at the first bottle, he became positively servile at the second. A third would have finished him, and my bank account. From the bill I learned that one bottle of Bass is equal to the wages of one able-bodied man working five days ; two bottles, the price of a donkey ; three bottles, no man can calculate.

Thus it is that a cruel government grinds the masses !

But the cutlet was tender and juicy, with just a dash of garlic ; the salad of lettuce of a wrinkled and many-seamed variety, with sprays of red pepper cut exceedingly fine and scattered through it, and, blessed be Bass ! the priceless bottles were full of the same old amber-colored nectar one always draws from under the same old compact, tinfoil-covered corks.

But to Guadaloupe and back before mass ended.

You reach this suburb of Zacatécas by a modern tramway which starts a car every hour; a sort of Mexican toboggan-slide, for the whole six miles is down hill by gravity. At the other end is the *Iglesia y Capilla de Guadaloupe,* — an exquisite modern chapel, — besides an old garden, a new market, a straggling suburb, and various teams of mules to toboggan you back again.

I stepped from the car and began sight-seeing. The chapel, the gift of a pious lady, is semi-oriental, with its creamy-white minarets shooting up from behind a mass of dark cedars relieved against the intense blue sky; the garden is overrun with sweet peas, poppies, calla lilies, and geraniums blooming amidst fleecy acacia-trees waving in the dazzling sunlight; the market has the usual collection of coarse pottery and green vegetables, with gay booths hung with bright zarapes and rebozos, and the straggling suburb is as picturesque and full of color as any other Mexican suburban village. I noted them all and each one, and they interested me intensely.

One other thing interested me infinitely more. It was an individual who came to my rescue in the midst of a dislocated Spanish sentence. I was at the moment in a curious old cloister adjoining the new chapel of Guadaloupe, examin-

ing with the aid of a rotund attendant the dia-
bolical pictures that lined its walls, when a tall,
well-built young fellow wearing a slouch hat
stopped immediately in front of the most repul-
sive canvas of the collection, and, after listening to my halting inquiry, supplied the missing
word in excellent Spanish. Then, shifting his
hat to the opposite ear, he pointed to the supposed portrait of an ancient martyr surrounded
by lurid flames behind iron bars, and remarked
quietly, —

" Beastly ugly old saint, is n't he ? Looks
like an underdone steak on a grill."

" You speak English, then ? "

" Why not ? You would n't want me to
cling to this jargon forever, would you ? "

From that instant the collection was forgotten.

He was about thirty years of age, with a
bronzed face, curling mustachios, and arching
eyebrows that shaded a pair of twinkling brown
eyes. A sort of devil-may-care air seemed to
pervade him, coupled with a certain recklessness discernible even in the way he neglected
his upper vest buttons, and tossed one end of
his cravat over his shoulder. He wore a large,
comfortable, easily adjusted slouch hat which
he kept constantly in motion, using it as some

75

men do their hands to emphasize their sen-
tences. If the announcement was somewhat
startling, the hat would be flattened out against
the back of his head, the broad brim standing
out in a circle, and framing the face, which
changed with every thought behind it. If of a
confidential nature, it was pulled down on the
side next to you like the pirate's in the play.
If his communication might offend ears polite,
he used one edge of it as a lady would a fan,
and, from behind it, gave you a morsel of scan-
dal with such point and pith that you forgave
its raciness because of the crisp and breezy way
with which it was imparted.

He hailed from New Orleans; had lived in Zacatécas two years; in western Mexico ten more;
was an engineer by profession; had constructed
part of the International Road, and was now
looking after some of its interests in Zacatécas.

"My name? Moon. Fits exactly, my dear
fellow, for I'm generally up all night. Been
here long?" He rattled on. "You ought to
stay a month. Richest town in all Mexico.
Just a solid silver mine under your feet all the
way from here to Zacatécas. Best people I
know anywhere, and more pretty girls to the
square mile than any spot on this terrestrial."

And then followed a running description of

his life here and at home, interspersed with various accounts of his scrapes and escapades, from which I gathered that he knew everybody in Zacatécas, including the priest, the commandant, and the pretty girl in the balcony. This biographical sketch was further enriched by such additional details as his once filling a holy father full of cognac to induce him to grant a right of way for a railroad through the convent garden ; of his being helped out of prison by the governor, who was his friend and who locked up his accuser ; and of his making love to a certain charming señorita whenever he got a chance, which, he declared, was now precious seldom, owing to a cross-eyed mother who saw both ways at once, and a duenna who hated him.

Would I take the tram and go back to Zacatécas with him ?

Yes, if he would stop at the cathedral at five and wait until vespers were over.

"So you have caught on, have you ? " Then in a confidential manner, "Come, now, give me her name. Reckon I know her. Bet it's the black-eyed girl with the high comb. She's always cutting her eye at the last stranger."

It was difficult to make this dare-devil of a Southerner understand that my engagement was entirely with a simple-minded, mild-eyed

old sacristan, and not with one of Zacatécas's
bewitching señoritas.

"What sacristan? Old Miguel? A greasy-
looking, bandy-legged old bald-head? Wears
a green jacket?"

I admitted that the description classified him
to some extent.

Moon broke out into a laugh that started the
six mules in a gallop up the tramway.

Did he know him? Well, he should think
so. Best post-office in Zacatécas, especially at
very early mass. What was he doing for me?
Smuggling letters?

No, buying a chair.

Moon laid one hand tenderly on my shoulder,
shifted his slouch hat over his right ear, and in
his peculiar vernacular characterized my statement as "diaphanous," and then in a coaxing
tone demanded the name of the girl.

"My friend, there *is* no girl. Wait until we
pass the cathedral. It is now five o'clock. The
sacristan is expecting me in the garden, and he
shall tell you the rest. There he is now, waiting under the palms."

"See here, Miguel," broke in Moon as we
alighted, ignoring the sacristan's obsequious
salutations. "What about this girl's chair?
Come, out with it."

78

Miguel looked at Moon and then turned to me and smiled grimly.

"It is always the señoritas with Señor Moon," he said, and then he repeated our interview of the morning, winding up with my incomprehensible infatuation for the four-legged relic, and his unsuccessful efforts with the padre to sell or exchange it for any number of new chairs, great or small.

"It is really impossible, señor painter. The padre says it is an old one of many years," continued the sacristan.

"If the painter wants the old ruin, he shall have it, you bow-legged old mailbag."

"The padre will not, Señor Moon ; not for ten new ones. I have exhausted everything."

"What padre ? " replied Moon.

"Padre Ignatius."

"Old Ig, is it ? No, he wouldn't part with an adobe brick." Then turning to me, " What did you tell him you wanted it for ? "

"For my studio."

"Studio be ——. Go, Miguel, and tell Padre Ignatius that my very old and very dear friend, the painter, is a devout Catholic from the holy city of New York; that he has an uncle, a holy father, in fact, a bishop, who is very poor, and who charged him to bring from the ancient

79

city of Zacatécas a sacred relic from this very
church, and that this aged, low-backed old cripple of a chair will exactly fill the bill. Go!
véte! But stop!" (In a lower tone.) "Did
you give it to her — the little one? When —
after early mass? *Bueno!*"

A long wait at the door of the sacristy; then
a footfall in the darkening twilight.

"Señor, the padre says he will consider. The
price is of course very small, and but that your
uncle the holy bishop is very poor it could not
be, but as a " —

"Hold up, Miguel. All right. Send the chair
to the painter's lodgings."

When I reached the church door and the
street and looked back, I could see the red towers of the cathedral gleaming pink and yellow
in the fading light of the afterglow, and far up
the crooked street I could hear my voluble friend
of an afternoon whistling an air from "Norma."

At the door of my lodgings I found the chair.

VI

IN THE CITY'S STREETS

NO one at all familiar with the history of Mexico can wander about the streets and suburbs of this its principal city without seeing at every turn some evidence of the vast changes which have marked its past, and which have made its story so thrilling.

If Prescott's pleasing fiction of Teocallis towering to the stars, the smoke of whose sacrifices curled upwards day and night; of gorgeous temples, of hanging and floating gardens, myriads of feather-clad warriors armed with spear and shield, swarms of canoes brilliant as tropical birds, and of a court surrounding Montezuma and Guatemotzin, more lavish than the wildest dream of the Orient, — if all this is true, — and I prefer to believe it rather than break the gods of my childhood, — so also are the great plaza of the cathedral, and the noble edifice itself with splendid façade and majestic twin towers, the hundreds of churches about which cluster the remains of convent, monastery, and hospital ; the wide paseos, the tropical gardens, the moss-bearded cypresses four centuries old, under which the disheartened Aztec monarch mourned the loss of his kingdom, the palaces of the viceroys, the alamedas and their fountains.

If you push aside the broad-leaved plants in the grand plaza, you will find heaped up and half covered with tangled vines the broken fragments of rudely carved stones, once the glory of an Aztec temple. If you climb down the steep hill under Chapultepec and break away the matted underbrush, you will discover the mutilated effigy of Ahuitzotl, the last of Montezuma's predecessors, stretched out on the natural rock, the same the ancient sculptor selected for his chisel in the days when the groves about him echoed with song, and when these same gnarled cypresses gave grateful shadow to priest, emperor, and slave.

Stroll out to Santa Anita ; examine the *chinampas*, the floating gardens of the old Mexican race. They are still there, overgrown with weeds and anchored by neglect. As in the old times, so now on every feast day the narrow canal of *las Vigas*, leading to the *chinampas*, is crowded with boats ; the maidens

82

bind wreaths of poppies about their heads, and the song and laughter of the light-hearted race — light-hearted when even for a day they lay their burdens down — still ring out in the twilight air.

The two civilizations, the pagan and the Christian, are still distinct to those who look below the surface. Time has not altered them materially. Even to-day in the hollows of the mountains and amid the dense groves on the tropical slopes the natives steal away and prostrate themselves before the stone images of their gods, and in the churches of the more remote provinces the parish priest has found more than once the rude sculptured idol concealed behind the Christian altar. To the kneeling peon the ugly stone is his sole hope of safety and forgiveness.

Important changes are taking place, however, which predict a happier future for Mexico. The monastery of San Hipólito, once the palace of Bucareli, now contains a printing press. The convent of Nuestra Señora de la Concepcion is a public school; the church of San Agustin, a public library ; and through the silent arches of many cloisters, and through many a secluded convent garden, run broad avenues filled with the gay life of the metropolis. Moreover to-day, every man, be he pagan, Christian, or Jew, may worship his particular god according to the dictates of his own conscience, in any form that pleases him.

Nothing so pointedly marks for me the strange contrasts which these changes have brought about, as my own quarters at the Hotel Jardin.

I am living in two rooms at the end of a long balcony overlooking a delicious garden, redolent with azaleas, pomegranates, and jasmine, in full bloom. I am at the extreme end of the balcony, which is several hundred feet long, and next to me is a stained and battered wall, encrusted with moss and lichen, supported by buttresses running sheer into the poppy beds. This wall sustains one side of a building which is surmounted by a quaint tile roof.

My rooms are high-ceiled and spacious, and floored with red brick. The walls, judged from the width of the door jambs, are of unusual strength.

At the other end of the balcony, from out the roof, rises a dome which glistens in the setting sun. It is covered with exquisite Spanish tiles of blue and yellow, each one of which forms part of a picture telling the story of the Cross. Beyond the garden, several squares away, cut sharp against the afternoon sky, curves the beautiful dome of the cathedral of San Francisco, beneath whose frescoed roof once rested the bones of Cortez.

Scarce twenty - five years ago the square bounded by this little dome with the Spanish tiles, this great dome of the cathedral, and the outside of the mould - stained convent wall, formed the great religious foundation of San Francisco, the richest and most powerful of the ecclesiastical holdings in Mexico. From this spot radiated the commanding influence of the order. Here masses were heard by Cortez. Here through three centuries the great festivals of the church were taken part in by the vice-roys. Here was sung the first Te Deum of Mexican independence, and here seventeen years later were held the magnificent funeral services of the liberator Yturbide.

How great the changes! To-day a Protestant congregation worships in the grand old cathedral, its interior a horror of whitewash and emptiness ; a modern hotel supplants the old infirmary and palace of the commissioners-general of the order ; a public livery stables its horses in the refectory, and four broad streets traverse the length and breadth of the sacred ground, irrespective of chancel, cloister, or garden. Through the top of the exquisite cupola surmounting the little glazed tile dome covering the chapel of San Antonio is thrust a sheet-iron stove-pipe. Within this once beautiful house of prayer, the space covered by the altar is now occupied by an enormous French range, upon which is ruined all the food of the Hotel Jardin. In the delightful arched windows, piles of dirty dishes replace the swinging lamps; near an exit where once stood the font, a plate-warmer of an Eastern pattern gives out an oily odor; and where the acolytes swung their censers, to-day swarms a perspiring mob of waiters urgent to be served by a *chef* who officiates in the exact spot where the holy archbishop celebrated high mass.

High on the cornice of the dome still clings the figure of San Domingo. His wooden bones and carved teeth should rattle and chatter themselves loose as he gazes down upon the awful sacrilege, for above him, where once the wings of the Dove of the Holy Spirit overspread the awe-hushed penitents, now twists with a convenient iron elbow a rusty pipe, that carries the foul breath of this impious range into the pure air of the heaven above.

As I sit on my section of the balcony and paint, I can see within a few yards of my easel

86

an open window, framed in the mouldy convent wall. The golden sunlight streams in, and falls upon the weather-stained stones and massive iron-bound shutter, touches a strip of dainty white curtain, and rests lovingly upon the head of a peon girl who sits all day sewing, and crooning to herself a quaint song. She watches me now and then with great wondering eyes. As I work I hear the low hum of a sewing-machine keeping time to her melody. Suddenly there is a quick movement among the matted leaves clinging to the festering wall, and from out a dark crevice creeps a slimy, snake-like lizard. He listens and raises his green head and glides noiselessly into the warm sunlight. There he stretches his lithe body and basks lazily.

I laid down my brushes, and fell into a reverie. The sunlight, the dark-eyed Indian girl, the cheery hum of her shuttle, and the loathsome lizard crawling from out the ruins of a dead convent wall told me the whole story of Mexico.

The old church of San Hipólito stands within a stone's throw of the spot where Alvarado, Cortez's greatest captain, is said to have made his famous leap on that eventful night of July 1, 1520, the Noche Triste. Indeed, it was built by one of the survivors of that massacre, Juan Garido, in commemoration of its horrors. Not

the present structure, but a little chapel of
adobe, which eighty years later was pulled
down to make room for the edifice of to-day.
You can still see upon the outside wall surrounding the atrium of the present building a
commemorative stone tablet, bearing the alto-
relievos of arms, trophies, and devices of the
ancient Mexicans, with this inscription : —

"So great was the slaughter of the Spaniards
by the Aztecs in this place on the night of July
1, 1520, named for this reason the Dismal
Night, that after having in the following year
reëntered the city triumphantly, the conquerors
resolved to build here a chapel, to be called the
Chapel of the Martyrs; and which should be
dedicated to San Hipólito, because the capture
of the city occurred upon that saint's day."

Janvier says: "Until the year 1812, there
was celebrated annually on the 13th of August
at this church a solemn ceremony, both religious
and civil, known as the Procession of the Banner (*Paseo del pendon*), in which the viceroy
and the great officers of the State and the nobility, together with the archbishops and dignitaries of the Church, took part. Its principal
feature was the carrying in state of the crimson
banner formerly borne by the conquerors, and
still preserved in the National Museum."

There was nothing to indicate the existence of any such ceremony the day I strolled into its quiet courtyard. The wooden gates, sagging and rotting on their hinges, were thrown back invitingly, but the broad flags of the pavement, overgrown with weeds and stubby grass thrust up between the cracks, showed but too plainly how few entered them.

Some penitents crossed the small inclosure in front of me, and disappeared within the cool doorway of the church. I turned to the left, hugged the grateful shadow of the high walls, reached the angle, opened my easel and began to paint.

It has a very dignified portal, this old church of San Hipólito, with half doors panelled and painted green, and with great whitewashed statues of broken-nosed saints flanking each side; and I was soon lost in the study of its ornament and color.

For a while nobody disturbed me or gave me more than a passing glance.

Presently I was conscious that an old fellow watering some plants across the court was watching me anxiously. When I turned again he stood beside me.

"Señor, why do you sit and look at the church ? "

"To take it home with me, *mi amigo.*"

"That cannot be. I will tell the padre."

He was gone before I could explain. In five minutes he returned, pale and trembling and without his hat. Behind him came an old priest with a presence like a benediction. Clinging to his hands were two boys, one with eyes like diamonds.

Before I could explain, the old man's face lighted up with a kindly smile, and he extended his hand.

"Nicolas is very foolish, señor. Do not mind him. Stay where you are. After service you can sit within the church and paint the interior, if you like. If the boys will not annoy you, please let them watch you. It will teach them something."

The little fellows did not wait for any further discussion. They both kissed his hand, and crept behind my easel. The youngest, with the diamond eyes, Pacheco, told me without drawing his breath his name, his age, where he went to school, that the good padre was his uncle, that his father had been dead forever almost, and that they lived across the way with their mother. The oldest stood by silently, watching every movement of my brush as if his life depended on it.

"And do you love the padre?" I asked, turning towards him.

"Yes." He replied in a quick, decided tone, as if it was a sacrilege to question it. "And so would you. Everybody, *everybody*, loves the padre."

"Is it not true?" This last to the sacristan, who had come out to see the painter, the service having begun.

The sacristan not only confirmed this, but gave me a running account of the misfortunes of the church even in his day, of its great poverty, of the changes he had seen himself. No more processions, no more grand masses; on Easter Sunday there was not even money enough to buy candles. He remembered a lamp as high as this wall that was stolen by the government, — this in a whisper behind his hand, — all solid silver, and a pair of candlesticks as big round as the tree yonder, all melted down to pay for soldiers. *Caramba!* It was terrible. But for the holy padre there would be no service at all. When the padre was young he lived in the priest's house and rode in his carriage. Now he is an old man, and must live with his sister over a posada. The world was certainly coming to an end.

I let the old sacristan ramble along, wishing

91

the service over, that I might see again the good padre whom everybody loved.

Soon the handful of people who, during the previous hour, had stolen in, as it were, one by one, crowded up the doorway and dispersed. It was a meagre gathering at best.

Then the old priest came out into the sunlight, and shaded his eyes with his hand, searching for me in the shadowed angle of the wall. As he walked across the court I had time to note the charming dignity of his manner, and the almost childlike smile that played across his features. His hair was silver white, his black frock faded and patched, though neatly kept, and his broad hat of a pattern and date of long ago. The boys sprang up, ran to him, caught him about the knees, and kissed his hands. Not as if it was a mark of devotion or respect, but as if they could not help it. The sacristan uncovered his head. For myself, I must confess that I was bareheaded and on my feet before I knew it. Would I come to his house and have a cup of coffee with him ? It was but across the street. The sacristan would see that my traps were not disturbed. At this the boys danced up and down, broke through the gate, and when we reached the narrow door that led to the balcony above, Pacheco had already dragged his

92

mother to the railing, to see the painter the good padre was bringing home.

It was a curious home for a priest. There were but three rooms, all fronting on a balcony of the second floor, overlooking a garden in which clothes were drying among and above the foliage. It was clean and cheery, however. Some pots of flowers bloomed in the windows, and there was a rocking-chair covered with a cotton cloth, a lounge with cushions, a few books and knickknacks, besides a square table holding a brass crucifix and two candles. In the corner of the adjoining room was an iron bedstead and a few articles of furniture. This was where the padre slept.

" The times are changed, good father ?" I asked, when he had finished filling his cup.

"Yes, my son, and for the worse." And then clearly but without bitterness, or any other feeling apparently, except the deepest sorrow, he told me the story of the downfall of his church in Mexico. It is needless to repeat it here. The old father thought only of the pomp, and splendor, and power for good, of the religion he loved, and could not see the degradation of the days he mourned. Within a stone's throw of where we sat the flowers were blooming, and the palms waving in the plaza of San Diego, over the exact spot where, less than a century ago, the smoke of the *auto de fé* curled away in the sunlight. I did not remind him of it. His own life had been so full of every good deed, and Christian charity, and all his own waking hours had been so closely spent either at altar or bedside, that he could not have understood how terrible could be the power of the church he revered, perverted and misused.

When he ceased he drew a deep sigh, rose from his chair, and disappeared into the adjoining room. In a few moments he returned, bearing in his arms a beautiful cope embroidered in silver on white satin.

"This, my son," said he, "is the last relic of value in San Hipólito. It is, as you see, very precious and very old. A present from Pope Innocent XII., who sent it to the brotherhood, the Hipólitos, in the year 1700. The pieces that came with it, the chasubles, stole, and other vestments, are gone. This I keep by my bedside."

He folded it carefully, returned it to its hiding-place, and accompanied me to the outer door. I can see him now, his white hair glistening in the light, the boys clinging to his hands.

94

VII

ON THE PASEO

THE English dogcart and the French bonnet have just broken out in the best society of Mexico. The disease doubtless came in with the railroads.

At present the cases are sporadic, and only the young caballero who knows Piccadilly and the gay señorita who has watched the brilliant procession pass under the Arc de Triomphe are affected. But it is nevertheless evident that in the larger cities the contagion is spreading, and that in a few years it will become epidemic.

Nowhere should the calamity of a change in national habits and costumes be more regretted than here. Stroll up the Paseo de la Reforma at sundown, — the Champs Elysées of Mexico, — and watch the endless procession of open carriages filled with beautiful women with filmy mantillas shading their dark eyes, the countless riders mounted on spirited horses, with saddle pommels hung with lasso and lariat; run your eye along the sidewalk thronged with people, and over the mounted soldiers in intermittent groups, policing the brilliant pageant, and tell me if anywhere else in the world you have seen so rich and novel a sight.

A carriage passes, and a velvet-eyed beauty in saluting an admirer drops her handkerchief. In an instant he wheels, dashes forward, and before you can think, he has picked up the dainty perfumed cambric from the dust without leaving his saddle, and all with the ease and grace of a Comanche.

Should a horse become unmanageable and plunge down the overcrowded thoroughfare, there are half a dozen riders within sight who can overtake him before he has run a stone's throw, loop a lasso over his head, and tumble him into the road. Not ranchmen out for an afternoon airing, but kid-gloved dandies in white buckskin and silver, with waxed mustaches, who learned this trick on the haciendas when they were boys, and to whom it is as easy as breathing. It is difficult to imagine any succeeding generation sitting back-a-back to a knee-breeched flunkey, and driving a curtailed cob before a pair of lumbering cart-wheels.

Analyze the features of a Spanish or Mexican beauty, — the purple-black hair, long drooping lashes, ivory - white skin, the sinking, half-swooning indolence of her manner. Note how graceful and becoming are the clinging folds of her mantilla, falling to the shoulders, and losing itself in the undulating lines of her exquisite figure. Imagine a cockchafer of a bonnet, an abomination of beads, bows, and bangles, surmounting this ideal inamorata. The shock is about as great as if some scoffer tied a seaside hat under the chin of the Venus de Milo.

Verily the illustrated newspaper and the ready-made clothing man have reduced the costume of the civilized and semi-barbarous world to the level of the commonplace ! I thank my lucky stars that I still know a few out-of-the-way corners where the castanet and high - heeled shoe, the long, flowing, many-colored tunic, the white sabot and snowy cap, and the sandal and sombrero, are still left to delight me with their picturesqueness, their harmony of color and grace.

All these reflections came to me as I strolled up the Reforma, elbowing my way along, avoiding the current, or crossing it for the shelter of one of the tree trunks lining the sidewalks, behind which I made five-minute outlines of the salient features of the moving panorama. When I reached the statue of Columbus, the

97

crowd became uncomfortable, especially that part which had formed a " cue," with the head looking over my sketch-book, and so I hailed a cab and drove away towards the castle of Chapultepec. The Paseo ends at this famous spot.

The fortress is built upon a hill that rises some two hundred feet above the valley, and is environed by a noble park and garden, above which tower the famous groves of hoary cypresses. On this commanding eminence once stood the palace of Montezuma, if we may believe the traditions. Indeed, Prescott dilates with enthusiasm upon the details of its splendor, and of its luxuriant adornment, these same cypresses playing an important part in the charming extravaganza with which he delighted our youth. The records say that when the haughty Spaniard knocked at the city's gate and demanded his person, his treasure, and his arms, the vacillating monarch retired to the cool shadows of these then ancient groves, collected together a proper percentage of his wives, and wept. This may be fiction, and that pious old monk, Bernal Diaz, Cortez's scribe, inspired by a lively sense of the value of his own head, and with a loyal desire to save his master's, may alone be responsible for it.

For this I care little. The trees are still here,

the very same old gnarled and twisted trunks.
The tawny Indian in feathers, the grim cavalier
in armor; fine ladies in lace; hidalgos in velvet, all the gay throngs who have enlivened
these shady aisles, each bedecked after the manner and custom of their times, are gone. But
the old trees still stand.

What the great kings of Tenochtitlan saw as
they looked up into their sheltering branches, I
see: the ribbed brown bark sparkling with gray
green lichen; the sweep of the wrinkled trunk
rushing upward into outspreading arms; the
clear sky turquoised amid matted foliage; the
gray moss waving in the soft air. With these
alive and above me, I can imagine the rest, and
so I pick out a particularly comfortable old root
that curves out from beneath one of the great
giants, and sit me down and persuade myself
that all the Aztec kings have been wont to rest
their bones thereon. From where I lounge, I
can see away up among the top branches the
castle and buildings of the military school, and
at intervals hear the bugle sounding the afternoon's drill. Later I toil up the steep ascent,
and from the edge of the stone parapet skirting
the bluff, drink in the glory and beauty of perhaps the finest landscape in the world.

There are two views which always rise up in

my memory when a grand panoramic vision bursts upon me suddenly. One is from a spot in the Sierra Nevada Mountains, in Granada, called "La Ultima Suspira de Mores." It is where Boabdil stood and wept when he looked for the last time over the beautiful valley of the Vega, — the loveliest garden in Spain, — the red towers and terraces of the Alhambra bathed in the setting sun. The other is this great sweep of plain and distant mountain range, with all its wealth of palm, orange, and olive ; the snow-capped twin peaks dominating the horizon; the silver line of the distant lakes; and the fair city, the Tenochtitlan of the ancient, the Eldorado of Cortez, sparkling like a jewel in the midst of this vast stretch of green and gold.

Both monarchs wept over their dominions,— Boabdil, that the power of his race which for six hundred years had ruled Spain was broken, and that the light of the Crescent had paled forever in the effulgence of the rising Cross; Montezuma, that the fires of his temples had forever gone out, and that henceforward his people were slaves.

Sitting here alone on this stone parapet, watching the fading sunlight and the long creeping shadows, and comparing Mexico and Spain of to-day with what we know to be true of the Moors, and what we hope was true of the Aztecs, and being in a reflective frame of mind, it becomes a question with me whether the civilized world ought not to have mingled their tears with both potentates. The delightful historian sums it up in this way: —

"Spain has the unenviable credit of having destroyed two great civilizations."

Full of these reveries, and with the question undecided, I retraced my steps past the boy sentinels, down the long hill, through the gardens and cypresses, and out into the broad road skirting the great aqueduct of Bucareli. There I hailed a cab, and whirled into the city brilliant with lights, and so home to my lodgings overlooking the old convent garden.

VIII

PALM SUNDAY IN PUEBLA DE LOS ANGELES

SOME one hundred miles from the city of Mexico, and within twice that distance of Vera Cruz and the sea, and some seven thousand feet up into the clear, crisp air, lies the city of Puebla. The streets are broad and clean, the plazas filled with trees and rich in flowers, the markets exceptionally interesting. Above this charming city tower, like huge sentinels, the two great volcanoes Popocatepetl and Iztaccihuatl.

The legend of its founding is quaint and somewhat characteristic; moreover, there is no shadow of doubt as to its truth.

The good Fray Julian Garces, the first consecrated bishop of the Catholic Church in Mexico, conceived the most praiseworthy plan of founding, somewhere between the coast and the city of Mexico, a haven of refuge and safe resting-place for weary travellers. Upon one eventful

night, when his mind was filled with this noble resolve, he beheld a lovely plain, bounded
by the great slope of the volcanoes, watered
by two rivers, and dotted by many ever-living
springs, making all things fresh and green. As
he gazed, his eyes beheld two angels, with line
and rod, measuring bounds and distances upon
the ground. After seeing the vision, the bishop
awoke, and that very hour set out to search for
the site the angels had shown him ; upon finding which he joyously exclaimed, " This is the
site the Lord has chosen through his holy angels, and here shall the city be ; " and even
now the most charming and delightful of all
the cities on the southern slope is this Puebla
de los Angeles. Nothing has occurred since to
shake confidence in the wisdom of the good
bishop, nor impair the value of his undertaking,
and to-day the idler, the antiquary, and the
artist rise up and call him blessed.

But the pious bishop did not stop here. As
early as 1536 he laid the corner-stone of the
present cathedral, completed one hundred and
fifty years later. This noble edifice, in its interior
adornments, lofty nave, broad aisles divided by
massive stone columns, inlaid floor of colored
marble, altars, chapels, and choirs, as well as
in its grand exterior, raised upon a terrace and

surmounted by majestic towers, is by far the most stately and beautiful of all the great buildings of Mexico.

Before I reached the huge swinging doors, carved and heavily ironed, I knew it was Palm Sunday; for the streets were filled with people, each one carrying a long, thin leaf of the sago palm, and the balconies crowded with children twisting the sacred leaves over the iron railings, to mark a blessing for the house until the next festival.

I had crossed the plaza, where I had been loitering under the trees, making memoranda in my sketch-book of the groups of Indians lounging on the benches in the shade, and sketching the outlines of bunches of little donkeys dozing in the sun ; and, mounting the raised terrace upon which the noble pile is built, found myself in the cool, incense-laden interior. The aisles were a moving mass of people waving palms over their heads, the vista looking like great fields of ferns in the wind. The service was still in progress, and the distant bursts of the organ resounded at intervals through the arches.

I wedged my way between the throngs of worshippers, — some kneeling, some shuffling along, keeping step with the crowd, — past the inlaid stalls, exquisite carvings, and gilded

figures of saints, until I reached the door of the
sacristy. I always search out the sacristy. It
contains the movable property of the church,
and as I have a passion for moving it, — when
the sacristan is of the same mind, — I always
find it the most attractive corner of any sacred
interior.

The room was superb. The walls were covered with paintings set in gilded frames ; the
chests of drawers were crammed with costly
vestments ; two exquisite tables covered with
slabs of onyx stood on one side, while upon
a raised shelf above them were ranged eight
superb Japanese Imari jars, — for water, I
presumed.

When I entered, a line of students near the
door were being robed in white starched garments by the sacristan ; groups of priests, in
twos and threes, some in vestments, others in
street robes, were chatting together on an old
settle ; and an aged, white-haired bishop was
listening intently to a young priest dressed in a
dark purple gown, — both outlined against an
open window. The whole effect reminded me of
one of Vibert's pictures. I was so absorbed that I
remained motionless in the middle of the room,
gazing awkwardly about. The next moment
the light was shut out, and I half smothered in

the folds of a muslin skirt. I had been mistaken for a student chorister, and the sacristan would have slipped the garment over my head but for my breathless protest. Had I known the service, I think I should have risked the consequences.

The sacristy opened into the chapter-room. The wanderer who thinks he must go to Italy to find grand interiors should stand at the threshold of this room and look in ; or, still better, rest his weary bones for half an hour within the perfectly proportioned, vaulted, and domed apartment, hung with Flemish tapestry and covered with paintings, and examine it at his leisure. He can select any one of the superb old Spanish chairs presented by Charles V., thirty-two of which line the walls ; then, being rested, he can step into the middle of the room, and feast his eyes upon a single slab of Mexican onyx covering a table large enough for a grand council of bishops. I confess I stood for an instant amazed, wondering whether I was really in Mexico, across its thousand miles of dust, or had wandered into some old palace or church in Verona or Padua.

At the far end of this chapter-room sat a grave-looking priest, absorbed in his breviary. I approached him, hat in hand.

"Holy father, I am a stranger and a painter. I know the service is in progress, and that I should not now intrude ; but this room is so beautiful, and my stay in Puebla so short, that I must crave your permission to enter."

He laid down his book. "*Mi amigo*, you are welcome. Wander about where you will, here and by the altar. You will disturb no one. You painters always revere the church, for within its walls your greatest works are held sacred."

I thought that very neat for a priest just awakened from a reverie, and, thanking him, examined greedily the superb old carved chair he had just vacated. I did revere the church, and told him so, but all the same I coveted the chair, and but for his compliment and devout air would have dared to open negotiations for its possession. I reasoned, iconoclast that I am, that it would hardly be missed among its fellows, and that perhaps one of those frightful renovations, constantly taking place in Mexican churches, might overtake this beautiful room, when new mahogany horrors might replace these exquisite relics of the sixteenth century, and the whole set be claimed by the second-hand man or the wood-pile.

Then I strolled out into the church with that vacant air which always marks one in a building new to him, — especially when it overwhelms him, — gazing up at the nave, reading the inscriptions under the pictures, and idling about the aisles. Soon I came to a confessional box. There I sat down behind a protecting column.

There is a fascination about the confessional which I can never escape. Here sits the old news-gatherer and safe-deposit vault of everybody's valuable secrets, peaceful and calm within the seclusion of his grated cabinet; and here come a troop of people, telling him all the good and bad things of their lives, and leaving with him for safe-keeping their most precious property, — their misdeeds. What a collection of broken bonds, dishonored names, and debts of ingratitude must he be custodian of!

The good father before me was a kindly-faced, plethoric old man; a little deaf, I should judge, from the fanning motion of his left hand, forming a sounding-board for his ear. About him were a group of penitents, patiently awaiting their turns. When I halted and sought the shelter of the pillar, the closely veiled and muffled figure of a richly dressed señora was bowed before him. She remained a few moments, and then slipped away, and another figure took her place at the grating.

I raised my eyes wistfully, wondering whether

I could read the old fellow's face, which was in strong light, sufficiently well to get some sort of an inkling of her confidences ; but no cloud of sorrow, or ruffle of anger, or gleam of curiosity passed over it. It was as expressionless as a harvest moon, and placid as a mountain lake. At times I even fancied he was asleep ; then his little eyes would open slowly and peep out keenly, and I knew he had only been assorting and digesting his several informations.

One after another they dropped away silently, — the Indian in his zarape, the old man in sandals, and the sad-faced woman with a black rebozo twisted about her throat. Each had prostrated himself, and poured through that six inches of space the woes that weighed heavy on his soul. The good father listened to them all. His patience and equanimity seemed marvellous.

I became so engrossed that I forgot I was an eavesdropper, and could make no sort of excuse for my vulgar curiosity which would satisfy any one upon whose privacy I intruded ; and, coming to this conclusion, was about to shoulder my trap and move off, when I caught sight of a short, thickset young Mexican, muffled to his chin in a zarape. He was leaning against the opposite column, watching earnestly the

same confessional box, his black, bead-like eyes
riveted upon the priest. In his hand he held a
small red cap, with which he partially concealed
his face. It was not prepossessing, the forehead being low and receding, and the mouth
firm and cruel.

As each penitent turned away, the man edged
nearer to the priest, with a movement that attracted me. It was like that of an animal slowly
yielding to the power of a snake. He was now
so close that I could see great drops of sweat
running down his temples; his breath came
thick and short; his whole form, sturdy fellow
as he was, trembled and shook. The cap was
now clenched in his fist and pressed to his breast,
— the eyes still fastened on the priest, and the
feet moving a few inches at a time. When the
last penitent had laid her face against the grating, he fell upon his knees behind her and buried
his face in his hands. When she was gone he
threw himself forward in her place and clutched
the grating with a moan that startled me.

I arose from my seat, edged around the pillar,
and got the light more clearly on the priest's
face. It was as calm and serene as a wooden
saint's.

For a few moments the Mexican lay in a heap
at the grating; then he raised his head, and

looked cautiously about him. I shrank into the shadow. The face was ghastly pale, the lips trembled, the eyes started from his head. The priest leaned forward wearily, his ear to the iron lattice. The man's lips began to move ; the confession had begun. Both figures remained motionless, the man whispering eagerly, and the priest listening patiently. Suddenly the good father started forward, bent down, and scanned the man's face searchingly through the grating. In another instant he uttered a half-smothered cry of horror, covered his face with the sleeve of his robe, and fell back on his seat.

The man edged around on his knees from the side grating to the front of the confessional, and bowed his head to the lower step of the box. For several minutes neither moved. I flattened myself against the column, and became a part of the architecture. Then the priest, with blanched face, leaned forward over the half door, and laid his hand on the penitent. The man raised his head, clutched the top of the half door, bent forward, and glued his lips to the priest's ear. I reached down noiselessly for my sketch-trap, peeled myself from the column as one would a wet handbill, and, keeping the pillar between me and the confessional, made a straight line for the sacristy.

III

Before I reached the door the priest overtook me, crossed the room, and disappeared through a smaller door in the opposite wall. I turned to avoid him, and caught sight of the red cap of the Mexican pressing his way hurriedly to the street. Waiting until he was lost in the throng, I drew a long breath, and dropped upon a bench.

The faces of both man and priest haunted me. I had evidently been the unsuspected witness of one of those strange confidences existing in Catholic countries between the criminal and the Church. I had also been in extreme personal danger. A crime so terrible that the bare recital of it shocked to demoralization so unimpressionable a priest as the good father was safe in his ear alone. Had there been a faint suspicion in the man's mind that I had overheard any part of his story, my position would have been dangerous.

But what could have been the crime? I reflected that even an inquiry looking towards its solution would be equally hazardous, and so tried to banish the incident from my mind.

A jar upon the other end of the bench awoke me from my reverie. A pale, neatly dressed, sad-looking young fellow had just sat down. He apologized for disturbing me, and the courtesy led to his moving up to my end.

" English ? "

" No, from New York."

" What do you sell ? "

" Nothing. I paint. This trap contains my canvas and colors. What do you do ? " I asked.

" I am a clerk in the Department of Justice. The office is closed to-day, and I have come into the church out of the heat, because it is cool."

I sounded him carefully, was convinced of his honesty, and related the incident of the confessional. He was not surprised. On the contrary, he recounted to me many similar instances in his own experience, explaining that it is quite natural for a man haunted by a crime to seek the quiet of a church, and that often the relief afforded by the confessional wrings from him his secret. No doubt my case was one of these.

" And is the murderer safe ? "

" From the priest, yes. The police agents, however, always watch the churches."

While we were speaking an officer passed, bowed to my companion, retraced his steps, and said, " There has been an important arrest. You may perhaps be wanted."

I touched the speaker's arm. " Pardon me. Was it made near the cathedral ? "

" Yes ; outside the great door."

" What was the color of his cap ? "

He turned sharply, looked at me searchingly, and said, lowering his voice, —

" Red."

A few days later I wandered into the market-place, in search of a subject. My difficulty was simply one of selection. I could have opened my easel at random and made half a dozen sketches without leaving my stool; but where there is so much wealth of material one is apt to be overcritical, and, being anxious to pick out the best, often loses the *esprit* of the first impression, and so goes away without a line. It was not the fault of the day or the market. The sun was brilliant beyond belief, the sky superb; the open square of the older section was filled with tumble-down bungalow-like sheds, hung with screens of patched matting; the sidewalks were fringed with giant thatched umbrellas, picturesque in the extreme; the costumes were rich and varied : all this and more, and yet I was not satisfied. Outside the slanting roofs, heaped up on the pavement, lay piles of green vegetables, pottery, and fruit, glistening in the dazzling light. Inside the booths hung festoons of bright stuffs, rebozos and *panuelos*, gray and cool by contrast. Thronging crowds of natives streamed in and out of the sheds, blocked up narrow passageways, grouped in the open, and disappeared into the black shadows of an inviting archway, beyond which an even crisper sunlight glowed in dabs, spots, and splashes of luxuriant color.

There was everything, in fact, to intoxicate a man in search of the picturesque, and yet I idled along without opening my sketch-book, and for more than an hour lugged my trap about: deciding on a group under the edge of the archway, with a glimpse of blue in the sky and the towers of the church beyond ; abandoning that instantly for a long stretch of street leading out of a square dotted with donkeys waiting to be unloaded ; and concluding, finally, to paint some high-wheeled carts, only to relinquish them all for something else.

I continued, I say, to waste thus foolishly my precious time, until, dazed and worn out, I turned on my heel, hailed a cab, and drove to the old Paseo. There I entered the little *plazuela*, embowered in trees, sat down opposite the delightful old church of San Francisco, and was at work in five minutes. When one is dazzled by a sunset, let him shut his eyes. After the blaze of a Mexican market, try the quiet grays of a seventeenth-century church, seen through soft foliage and across cool, shady walks.

This church of San Francisco is another of the delightful old churches of Puebla. I regret that the fiend with the bucket and the flat brush has practically destroyed almost the whole interior except the choir, which is still exquisite with its finely carved wooden stalls and rich organ; but I rejoice that the outside, with its quaint altar fronting on the *plazuela* façade of dark brick ornamented with panels of Spanish tiles, stone carvings, statues, and lofty towers, is still untouched, and hence beautiful.

Adjoining the church is a military hospital and barracks, formerly an old convent. I was so wholly wrapped up in my work that my water-cup needed refilling before I looked up and about me. To my surprise, I was nearly surrounded by a squad of soldiers and half a dozen officers. One fine-looking old fellow, with gray mustache and pointed beard, stood so close that my elbow struck his knee when I arose.

The first thought that ran through my head was my experience of Sunday, and my unpardonable imprudence in imparting my discoveries of the confessional to the sad-faced young man on the bench. Tracked, of course, I concluded, — arrested in the streets, and held as a witness on bread and pulque for a week. No passport, and an alibi out of the question ! A second glance reassured me. The possessor of the pointed beard only smiled cordially, apologized, and seated himself on the bench at my right. His intentions were the most peaceful. It was the growing picture that absorbed him and his fellow officers and men. They had merely deployed noiselessly in my rear, to find out what the deuce the stranger was doing under that white umbrella. Only this, and nothing more.

I was not even permitted to fill my water-bottle. A sign from my friend, and a soldier, with his arm in a sling, ran to the fountain, returned in a flash, and passed the bottle back to me with so reverential an air that but for the deep earnestness of his manner I should have laughed aloud. He seemed to regard the water-bottle as the home of the witch that worked the spell.

After that the circle was narrowed, and my open cigarette case added a touch of good fellowship, everybody becoming quite cosey and sociable. The officer was in command of the barracks. His brother officers — one after another was introduced with much form and manner — were on duty at the hospital except one, who was in command of the department of police of the city. A slight chill ran down my spine, but

117

I returned the commandant's bow with a smile that established at once the absolute purity of my life.

For two hours, in the cool of the morning, under the trees of the little *plaçuela*, this charming episode continued ; I painting, the others around me deeply interested ; all smoking, and chatting in the friendliest possible way. At the sound of a bugle the men dropped away, and soon after all the officers bowed and disappeared, except my friend with the pointed beard and the commandant of the police. These two moved their bench nearer, and sat down, determined to watch the sketch to the end.

The conversation drifted into different channels. The system of policing the streets at night was explained to me, the manner of arrest, the absolute authority given to the *jefe politico* in the rural districts, — an execution first, and an investigation afterwards, — the necessity for such prompt action in a country abounding in bandits, the success of the government in suppressing the evil, etc.

" And are the crimes confined wholly to the country districts ? " I asked. " Are your cities safe ? "

"Generally, yes. Occasionally there is a murder among the lower classes of the people.

It is not always for booty ; revenge for some real or fancied injury often prompts it."

" Has there been any particularly brutal crime committed here lately ? " I asked carelessly, skirting the edge of my precipice.

" Not exactly here. There was one at At- lixco, a small town a few miles west of here, but the man escaped."

" Have you captured him ? "

" Not yet. There was a man arrested here a few days ago, who is now awaiting examina- tion. It may be that we have the right one. We shall know to-morrow."

I kept at work, dabbing away at the mass of foliage, and putting in pats of shadow tones.

" Was it the man arrested near the cathe- dral on Palm Sunday ? "

" There was a man arrested on Palm Sun- day," he replied slowly. " How did you know ? "

I looked up, and found his eyes riveted on me in a peculiar, penetrating way.

" I heard it spoken of in the church," I re- plied, catching my breath. My foot went over the precipice. I could see into the pit below.

" If the American heard of it," said he in a low voice, turning to my friend, " it was badly done."

I filled a fresh brush with color, leaned over my canvas, and before I looked up a second time had regained my feet and crawled back to a safe spot. — I could hear the stones go rumbling down into the abyss beneath me. Then I concentrated myself upon the details of the façade, and the officer began explaining the early history of the founding of the church, and the many vicissitudes it had experienced in the great battles which had raged around its towers. By the time he had finished the cold look went out of his eyes.

The sketch was completed, the trap bundled up, three hats were raised, and we separated.

I thought of the horror-stricken face of the priest and the crouching figure of the Mexican ; then I thought of that penetrating, steel-like glance of the commandant.

So far as I know, the priest alone shares the secret.

IX

A DAY IN TOLUCA

HITHERTO my travels, with the exception
of a divergence to Puebla, have been in
a straight line south, beginning at the frontier
town of El Paso, stopping at Zacatécas, Aguas
Calientes, Silao, Guanajuato, and Querétaro,
— all important cities on the line of the Mexican Central Railroad, — and ending at the city
of Mexico, some twelve hundred miles nearer
the equator.

It is true that I have made a flying trip over
the Mexican Railway, passing under the shadow
of snow-capped Orizaba, have looked down into
the deep gorges of the *Infiernillo*, reeking with
the hot, humid air of the tropics, and have spent
one night in the fever-haunted city of Vera
Cruz; but my experiences were confined to
such as could be enjoyed from the rear platform of a car, to a six by nine room in a stuffy
hotel, and to a glimpse at night of the sea,

impelled by a norther, rolling in from the Gulf and sousing the quay incumbered with surf boats. Had I been a bird belated in the autumn, I could have seen more.

This bright April morning I have shaken the dust of the great city from my feet, and have bent my steps westward towards the Pacific. In common parlance, I have bought a first-class ticket for as far as the national railroad will take me, and shall come bump up against the present terminus at Pátzcuaro.

On my way west I shall stop at Toluca, an important city some fifty miles down the road, tarry a while at Morelia, the most delightful of all the cities of western Mexico, and come to a halt at Pátzcuaro, — in all some three hundred miles from where I sit in the station and look out my car window. I am particular about these distances.

At Pátzcuaro I shall find a lake bearing the same name. Up this lake, nearly to the end, an Indian adobe village ; at the end of the village a tumbling-down church and convent, within this convent a cloister, leading out of the cloister a narrow passage ending in a low-ceiled room with its one window protected by an iron grating. Through this fretwork of rusty iron the light streams in, falling, I am told, upon one of

the priceless treasures of the world — an Entombment by Titian.

This, if you please, is why my course points
due west.

The scenery along the line of the road from
the city of Mexico to where the divide is
crossed at *la Cima* — some ten thousand feet
above the level of the sea, and thence down
into the Toluca Valley — was so inexpressibly
grand that I was half the time in imminent danger of decorating a telegraph pole with my head,
in my eagerness to enjoy it.

Great masonry dams hold back lakes of silver shimmering in the sunlight; deep gorges lie
bottomless in purple shadows; wide stretches
of tableland end in volcanoes, ragged, dead, and
creviced with snow; and sharp craggy peaks,
tumbling waterfalls, and dense semi-tropical
jungles start up and out and from under me at
every curve.

On reaching the valley of Toluca, the road,
as it nears the red-tiled roofs of the city, follows
the windings of the river Lerma, its banks
fringed with natives bathing. On reaching the
city itself the clean, well-dressed throng at the
depot explains at a glance the value of this
stream apart from its irrigating properties.

And the city is clean, with a certain well-planned, well-built, and orderly air about it, and quite a modern air too. Remembering a fine gray dust which seems to be a part of the very air one breathes, and the great stretches of gardens filled with trees, and the long drought continuing for months, I should say that the prevailing color of Toluca's vegetation is a light mullein-stalk green. Then the houses are a dusty pink, the roofs a dusty red, and the streets and sidewalks a dusty yellow, and the sky always and ever, from morn till night, a dusty blue. It is the kind of place Cazin, the great French impressionist, would revel in. So subtle and exquisite are the grays and their harmonies that one false note from your palette sets your teeth on edge.

But Toluca is not by any means a modern city, despite its apparent newness, its air of prosperity, and its generally brushed-up appearance. It is one of the oldest of the Spanish settlements. No less a personage than the great Cortez himself received its site, and a comfortable slice of the surrounding country thrown in, as a present from his king. In fact it is but a few years, not twenty, since the government pulled down the very house once occupied by the conqueror's son, Don Martin Cortez, and built upon its site the present imposing state buildings fronting the plaza *major*.

This pulling down and rebuilding process is quite fashionable in Toluca, and has extended even to its churches. The primitive church of San Francisco was replaced by a larger structure of stone in 1585, and this in turn by an important building erected in the seventeenth century; and yet these restless people, as if cramped for room, levelled this edifice to the ground in 1874 and started upon its ruins what purposes to be a magnificent temple, judging from the acres it covers. In fourteen years it has grown twelve feet high. Some time during the latter part of the next century they will be slating the roof.

Then there are delightful markets, and a fine bull-ring, and in the suburbs a pretty alameda full of matted vines and overgrown walks, besides two gorgeous theatres. Altogether Toluca is quite worth visiting, even if it does not look as old as the Pyramids or as dilapidated as an Arab town.

In all this newness there is one spot which refreshes you like a breeze from afar. It is the little chapel of Nuestra Señora del Carmen, laden with the quaintness, the charm, and the dust of the sixteenth century. It has apparently never yet occurred to any Tolucan to retouch it, and my only fear in calling attention to it now is, that during the next annual spring cleaning the man with the bucket will smother its charm in whitewash.

It was high noon when I sallied out from my lodgings to look for this forgotten relic of the past. I had spent the morning with that ubiquitous scapegrace Moon, whom I had met in Zacatécas some weeks before and who had run up to Toluca on some business connected with the road. He nearly shook my arm off when he ran against me in the market, inquired after the chair, vowed I should not wet a brush until I broke bread with him, and would have carried me off bodily to breakfast had I not convinced him that no man could eat two meals half an hour apart. He was delighted that I could find nothing, as he expressed it, " rickety " enough to paint in Toluca, and then relenting led me up to a crack in a crooked street, pointed ahead to the chapel, and deserted me with the remark, —

"Try that. It is as musty as a cheese and about a million years old."

I passed through a gate, entered the sacred building, and wandered out into a patio, or sort of cloister. Instantly the world and its hum were gone. It was a small cloister, square, paved with marble flags, and open to the blue sky

126

above. Beneath the arches, against the wall, hung a few paintings, old and weather-stained. Opposite from where I stood was an open door. I crossed the quadrangle and entered a cosily furnished apartment. The ceiling was low and heavily beamed, the floor laid in brick tiles, and the walls faced with shelves loaded with books bound in vellum with titles labelled in ink.

Over the door was an unframed picture, evidently a Murillo, and against the opposite wall hung several large copies of Ribera. In one corner under a grated window rested an iron bedstead, — but recently occupied, — and near it an armchair with faded velvet cushions. A low table covered with books and manuscripts, together with a skull, candle, and rosary, a copper basin and pitcher, and a few chairs, completed the interior comforts. Over the bed, within arm's reach, hung a low shelf, upon which stood a small glass cup holding a withered rose. The cup was dry and the flower faded and dust-covered.

A second and smaller room opened out to the left. I pushed aside the curtains and looked in. It was unoccupied, like the first. As I turned hurriedly to leave the apartments my eye fell upon a copy of Medina's works bound in vellum, yellow and crinkled, the backs tied by a leathern string. I leaned forward to note the date. Suddenly the light was shut out, and from the obstructed doorway came a voice quick and sharp.

"What does the stranger want with the padre's books?" I looked up and saw a man holding a bunch of keys. The situation was unpleasant. Without changing my position, I lifted the book from the shelf and carefully read the title-page.

"Will he be gone long?" I answered, slowly replacing the volume.

"You are waiting, then, for Fray Geronimo? Many pardons, señor; I am the sacristan. I will find the padre and bring him to you."

I sank into the armchair. Retreat now was impossible. This will do for the sacristan, I thought, but how about the priest?

In a moment more I caught the sound of quickening footsteps crossing the patio. By the side of the sacristan stood a bareheaded young priest, dressed in a white robe which reached to his feet. He had deep-set eyes, which were intensely dark, and a skin of ivory whiteness. With a kindly smile upon his handsome, intellectual face, he came forward and said, —

"Do you want me?"

I laid my course in an instant.

128

"Yes, holy father," I replied, rising, "to crave your forgiveness. I am an American and a painter ; see, here is my sketch-book. I entered your open door, believing it would lead me to the street. The Murillo, the Riberas, the wonderful collection of old books, more precious than any I have ever seen in all Mexico, overcame me. I love these things, and could not resist the temptation of tarrying long enough to feast my eyes."

"*Mi amigo*, do not be disturbed. It is all right. You can go, Pedro," — this to the sacristan. "I love them too. Let us look them over together."

For more than an hour we examined the contents of the curious library. Almost without an exception each book was a rare volume. There were rows of ecclesiastical works in Latin with red-lettered title-pages printed in Antwerp; two editions of Don Quixote with copper plates, published in Madrid in 1760, besides a varied collection of the early Mexican writers, including Alarcon, the dramatist, and Gongora, the poet-philosopher.

Then in the same gracious manner he mounted a chair and took from the wall the unframed Murillo, "A Flight into Egypt," and placed it in the light, saying that it had formerly belonged to an ancestor and not to the church, and that believing it to be the genuine work of the great master, he had brought it with him when he came to Toluca, the face of the Madonna being especially dear to him. Next he unlocked a closet and brought me an ivory crucifix of exquisite workmanship, the modelling of the feet and hands recalling the best work of the Italian school. He did not return this to the closet, but placed it upon the little shelf over his bed, close to the dry cup which held the withered rose. In the act the flower slipped from the glass. Noticing how carefully he moved the cup aside, and how tenderly he replaced the shrivelled bud, I said laughingly, —

"You not only love old books, but old flowers as well."

He looked at me thoughtfully, and replied gravely, —

"Some flowers are never old."

In the glare of the sunlight of the street I met Moon. He had been searching for me for an hour.

"Did you find that hole in the wall?" he called out. "Come over here where the wind can blow through you. You must feel like a grave-digger. Where is your sketch?"

I had no sketch and told him so. The interior was in truth delightfully picturesque, but the young priest was so charming that I had not even opened my trap.

"What sort of a looking priest?"

I described him as closely as I could.

"It sounds like Geronimo. Yes — same priest."

"Well — ?"

"Oh! the old story, and a sad one. Gray dawn — muffled figures — obliging duenna — diligence — governor on horseback — girl locked up in a hacienda — student forced into the Church. Queer things happen in Mexico, my boy, and *cruel* ones too."

X

TO MORELIA WITH MOON

MOON insists on going to Morelia with me. He has a number of reasons for this sudden resolve : that the señoritas are especially charming and it is dangerous for me to go alone ; that he knows the sacristan *major* of the cathedral and can buy for me for a song the entire movable property of the church ; that there is a lovely alameda overgrown with wild roses, and that it is so tangled up and crooked I will lose the best part of it if he does not pilot me about ; and finally, when I demur, that he has received a despatch from his chief to meet him in Morelia on the morrow, and he must go anyhow.

He appears the next morning in a brown linen suit, with the same old sombrero slanted over one eye, and the loose end of his necktie tossed over his shoulder. On the way to the station he holds a dozen interviews with citizens occupying balconies along the route. He generally conducts these from the middle of the street, pitching his voice to suit the elevation. Then he deflects to the sidewalk, runs his head into the door of a posada, wakes up the inmates with a volley of salutations, bobs out again, hails by name the driver of a tram, and when he comes to a standstill calls out that he has changed his mind and will walk, and so arrives at the station bubbling over with good humor, and as restless as a schoolboy.

I cannot help liking this breezy fellow, despite his piratical air, his avowed contempt for all the laws that govern well-regulated society, and his professed unbelief in the sincerity of everybody's motives.

His acquaintance is marvellous. He knows everybody, from the water-carrier to the archbishop. He speaks not only Spanish, but half a dozen native dialects picked up from the Indians while he was constructing the railroad. He has lived in every town and village on the line; knows Morelia, Pátzcuaro, Tzintzúntzan, and the lake as thoroughly as he does his own abiding-place at Zacatécas; is perfectly familiar with all the mountain trails and short cuts across plains and foothills; is a born tramp, the best of Bohemians, and the most entertaining travelling companion possible.

His baggage is exceedingly limited. It consists of a tooth-brush, two collars, and a bundle of cigars. He replies to my remarks on its compactness, that "anybody's shirts fit him, and that he has plenty of friends up the road." And yet with all this there is something about the fearless way in which he looks you straight in the eye, and something about the firm lines around his mouth, that, in spite of his devil-may-care recklessness, convinces you of his courage and sincerity.

"Crawl over here," he breaks out from the end of the car, "and see this hacienda. Every square acre you see, including that range of mountains, belongs to one Mexican. It covers exactly one hundred and twenty square miles. The famished pauper who owns it has taken five millions of dollars from it during the last fifteen years. For the next eighteen miles you will ride through his land."

"Does he live here?" I inquired.

"No, he knows better. He lives in Paris like a lord, and spends every cent of it."

We were entering the lake country, and caught glimpses of Cuitzo shimmering through the hills.

"These shores are alive with wild fowl," continued Moon; "there goes a flight of stork,

134

now. You can bag a pelican and half a dozen flamingoes any morning along here before break-fast. But you should see the Indians hunt. They never use a gun when they go ducking. They tie a sharp knife to a long pole and spear the birds as they fly over. When they fish they strew green boughs along the water's edge, and when the fish seek the shade, scoop them up with a dip-net made from the fibre of the pulque plant. This country has changed but little since that old pirate Cortez took pos-session of it, as far as the Indians go. Many of them cannot understand a word of Spanish now, and I had to pick up their jargon myself, when I was here."

" Hello, Goggles !" he shouted out, suddenly jumping from his seat as the train stopped. I looked out and saw a poor blind beggar, guided by a boy with a stick.

" I thought you were dead long ago."

In a moment more he was out of the train and had the old man by the hand. When he turned away, I could see by the way the blind face lighted up that he had made him the richer in some way. The boy too seemed overjoyed, and would have left his helpless charge in the push-ing crowd but for Moon, who snatched away the leading stick, and placed it in the beggar's hand

again. Then he fell to berating the boy for his
carelessness, without, however, diminishing in
the least the latter's good humor, raising his
voice until the car windows were filled with
heads.

All this in a dialect that was wholly unintel-
ligible.

"You know the beggar," I remarked.

"Of course; old Tizapan. Lost his eyes
digging in a silver mine. That little devil is his
grandson. If I had my way I would dig a hole
and fill it up with these cripples."

When we reached Morelia it was quite dark,
and yet it was difficult to get Moon out of the
station, so many people had a word to say to
him. When we arrived at the hotel fronting the
plaza he was equally welcome, everybody greet-
ing him.

It was especially delightful to see the landlord. He first fell upon his neck and embraced
him, then stood off at a distance and admired
him, with his arms akimbo, drinking in every
word of Moon's raillery. At the bare mention
of dinner, he rushed off and brought in the cook,
whom Moon addressed instantly as Griddles,
running from Spanish into English and French,
and back again into Spanish, in the most surprising way.

"We will have a Mexican dinner for the painter, Griddles ! No *bon bouche*, but a square meal, *un buena comida ! magnifica !* especially some little fish baked in corn-husks, peppers stuffed with tomatoes with plenty of *chile*, an onion salad with garlic, stewed figs, and a cup of Uruápam coffee, — the finest in the world," — this last to me.

Later all these were duly served and deliciously cooked, and opened my eyes to the resources of a Mexican kitchen when ordered by an expert.

In the morning Moon started for his friend the sacristan. He found him up a long flight of stone steps in one end of the cathedral. But he was helpless, even for Moon. We must find Padre Bailo, who lived near the Zocolo. He had the keys and charge of all the worn-out church property. Another long search across plazas and in and out of market stalls, and Padre Bailo was encountered leaving his house on his way back to the cathedral. But it was impossible. *Mañana por la mañana,* or perhaps next week, but not to-day. Moon took the dried-up old fossil aside, and brought him back in five minutes smiling all over, with a promise to unlock everything on my return from Pátzcuaro.

"Now for the alameda. It is the most delightful old tangle in Mexico : rose-trees as high as a house ; by-paths overgrown with vines and lost in beds of violets ; stone benches galore ; through the centre an aqueduct so light it might be built of looped ribbons; and such señoritas ! I met a girl under one of those arches who would have taken your breath away. She had a pair of eyes, and a foot, and " —

" Never mind what the girl had, Moon. We may find her yet on one of the benches and I will judge for myself. Show me the alameda."

" Come on, then."

At the end of a beautiful street nearly half a mile long, — in reality a raised stone causeway with stone parapets and stone benches on either side, and shaded its entire length by a double row of magnificent elms, — I found the abandoned Paseo de las Lechugas (the street of the Lettuces).

Moon had not exaggerated the charm of its surroundings. Acacias and elms interlaced their branches across the walks, roses ran riot over the stone benches, twisted their stems in and out of the railings, and tossed their blossoms away up in the branches of the great trees. High up against the blue, the graceful aqueduct stepped along on its slender legs, trampling the high grass, and through and into and over all, the afternoon sun poured its flood of gold.

The very unkempt, deserted air of the place added to its beauty. It looked as if the forces of nature, no longer checked, had held high revel, and in their glee had well-nigh effaced all trace of closely cropped hedge, rectangular flower-bed, and fantastic shrub. The very poppies had wandered from their beds and stared at me from the roadside with brazen faces, and the once dignified tiger lilies had turned tramps and sat astride of the crumbling curbs, nodding gayly at me as I passed.

"Did I not tell you?" broke out Moon. "How would you like to be lost in a tangle like this for a month with a Fatinitza all eyes and perfume, with little Hottentots to serve you ices, and fan you with peacock tails?"

I admitted my inability to offer any valid objection to any such delicious experience, and intimated that, but for one obstacle, he could bring on his Hottentots and trimmings at once — I was *en route* for Pátzcuaro, Tzintzúntzan, and the Titian.

This was news to Moon. He had expected Pátzcuaro, that being the terminus of the greatest railroad of the continent, — P. Moon, civil engineer, — but why any sane man wanted to

139

wander around looking for a dirty adobe Indian village like Tzintzúntzan, away up a lake, with nothing but a dug-out to paddle there in, and not a place to put your head in after you landed, was a mystery to him. Besides, who said there was any Titian ? At all events, I might stay in Morelia until I could find my way around alone. The Titian had already hung there three hundred years ; he thought it would hold out for a day or two longer.

So we continued rambling about this most delightful of all the Mexican cities ; across the plaza of La Paz at night ; sitting under the trees listening to the music, and watching the love-making on the benches ; in the cathedral at early mass, stopping for fruit and a cup of coffee at the market on the way ; through the college of San Nicholas, where Fray Geronimo had studied ; to the governor's house to listen to a concert and to present ourselves to his excellency, who had sent for us ; to the great pawn-shop, the Monte de Piedad, on the regular day of sale, and to the thousand and one delights of this *dolce far niente* city, — returning always at sundown to the inn, to be welcomed by the landlord, who shouted for Griddles the moment he laid eyes on Moon, and began spreading the cloth on the little table under the fig-tree in the garden.

After this Bohemian existence had lasted for several days I suddenly remembered that Moon had not been out of my sight five waking minutes, and being anxious for his welfare, I ventured to jog his memory.

"Moon, did you not tell me that you came here on orders from your chief, who wanted you on urgent business and was waiting for you ? "

" Yes."

" Have you seen him ? "

" No."

" Heard from him ? "

" No."

" What are you going to do about it ? "

" Let him wait."

XI

PÁTZCUARO AND THE LAKE

WHEN I rapped at Moon's door the next morning he refused to open it. He apologized for this refusal by roaring through the transom that the thought of my leaving him alone in Morelia had caused him a sleepless night, and that he had determined never to look upon my face again; that he had " never loved a dear gazelle," etc., — this last sung in a high key; that he was not coming out; and that I might go to Pátzcuaro and be hanged to me.

So the landlord and Griddles escorted me to the station, the *chef* carrying my traps, and the landlord a mysterious basket with a suggestive bulge in one corner of the paper covering. As the train moved slowly out, this basket was passed through the window with a remark that Mr. Moon had prepared it the night before, with especial instructions not to deliver it until I was under way. On removing the covering the bulge

142

proved to be glass, with a tinfoil covering the cork, on top of which was a card bearing the superscription of my friend, with a line stating that "charity of the commonest kind had influenced him in this attempt to keep me from starving during my idiotic search for the Titian, that the dulces beneath were the pride of Morelia, the fruit quite fresh, and the substratum of sandwiches the best Griddles could make."

I thanked the cheery fellow in my heart, forgave him his eccentricities, and wondered whether I should ever see his like again.

An hour later I had finished the customary inventory of the car: the padre, very moist and very dusty, as if he had reached the station from afar, mule-back; the young Hidalgo with buckskin jacket, red sash, open-slashed buckskin breeches with silver buttons of bulls' heads down the seam, wide sombrero, and the ivory handle of a revolver protruding from his hip pocket; the two demure señoritas dressed in black with veils covering their heads and shoulders, attended by the stout duenna on the adjoining seat, with fat, pudgy hands, hoop earrings, and restless eyes; the old Mexican, thin, yellow, and dried up, with a cigarette glued to his lower lip.

I had looked them all over carefully, speculating as one does over their several occupations and antecedents, and feeling the loss of my encyclopædic friend in unravelling their several conditions, when the door of the car immediately in front of me opened, and that ubiquitous individual himself slowly sauntered in, his cravat flying, and his big sombrero flattened against the back of his head. The only change in his costume had been the replacing of his brown linen suit with one of a fine blue check, newly washed and ironed in streaks. From his vest pocket protruded his customary baggage, — the ivory handle and the points of two cigars.

" Why, Moon ! " I blurted out, completely surprised. " Where did you come from ? "

" Baggage car — had a nap. Got the basket, I see."

"I left you in bed," I continued.

" You did n't. Was shivering on the outside, waiting for the landlord's clothes. How do they fit ? Left mine to be washed."

" Where are you going ? " I insisted, determined not to be side-tracked.

" To Pátzcuaro." Then with a merry twinkle in his eye he leaned forward, canted his sombrero over his left eye, and shading his mouth with its brim whispered confidentially, " You see, I got a dispatch from my chief to meet him in Pátzcuaro, and I managed by hurrying a little to catch this train."

Pátzcuaro lies on a high hill overlooking the lake. The beautiful sheet of water at its foot, some twenty miles long and ten wide, is surrounded by forest-clad hills and studded with islands, and peopled almost exclusively by Indians, who support themselves by fishing.

The town is built upon hilly broken ground, the streets are narrow and crooked, and thoroughly Moorish in their character, and the general effect picturesque in the extreme.

On alighting from the train it was evident that the progressiveness of the nineteenth century ended at the station. Drawn up in the road stood a lumbering stage-coach and five horses. It was as large as a country barn, and had enormous wheels bound with iron and as heavy as an artillery wagon's. In front there hung a boot made of leather an inch thick, with a multitude of straps and buckles. Behind, a similar boot, with more straps and buckles. On top was fastened an iron railing, protecting an immense load of miscellaneous freight. There was also a flight of steps that let down in sections, with a hand-rail to assist the passenger. Within and without, on cushions, sides, curtains, over top, baggage, wheels, driver, horses, and harness the gray dust lay in layers, — not sifted over it, but piled up in heaps.

The closest scrutiny on my companion's part failed to reveal the existence of anything resembling a spring, made either of leather, rawhide, or steel. This last was a disappointment to Moon, who said that occasionally some coaches were built that way.

But two passengers entered it, — Moon and I; the others, not being strangers, walked. The distance to the town from the station is some two miles, up hill. It was not until my trap rose from the floor, took a flying leap across the middle of the seat, and landed edgewise below Moon's breastbone, that I began fully to realize how badly the authorities had neglected the highway. Moon coincided, remarking that they had evidently blasted it out in the rough, but the pieces had not been gathered up.

We arrived first, entering the arcade of the Fonda Concordia afoot, the coach lumbering along later minus half its top freight.

A cup of coffee, — none better than this native coffee, — an omelet with peppers and some fruit, and Moon started out to make arrangements for my trip up the lake to Tzintzúntzan and the Titian, and I with my sketch-book to see the town.

146

A closer view was not disappointing.

Pátzcuaro is more Moorish than any city in Mexico. The houses have overhanging eaves supported by roof rafters similar to those seen in southern Spain. The verandas are shaded by awnings and choked up with flowers. The arcades are flanked by slender Moorish columns, the streets are crossed by swinging lanterns stretched from house to house by iron chains, the windows and doorways are surmounted by the horseshoe arch of the Alhambra, and the whole place inside and out reminds you of Toledo transplanted. Although seven thousand feet above the level of the sea, it is so near the edge of the slope running down into the hot country that its market is filled with tropical fruits unknown on the plateau of Mexico farther east, and the streets thronged with natives dressed in costumes never met with in high latitudes.

Tradition has it that in the days of the good Bishop Quiroga, when the See of Michoacan was removed hither from Tzintzúntzan, Pátzcuaro gave promise of being an important city, as is proved by the unfinished cathedral. When, however, the See was again removed to Morelia the town rapidly declined, until to-day it is the least important of the old cities of Michoacan.

The plaza is trodden down and surrounded by market stalls, the churches are either abandoned or, what is worse, renovated, and there is nothing left of interest to the idler and antiquary, outside of the charm of its picturesque streets and location, except, it may be, the tomb of the great bishop himself, who lies buried under the altar of the Jesuit church, the Campañia, — his bones wrapped in silk.

I made some memoranda in my sketch-book, bought some coffee, lacquer ware, and feather work, and returned to the inn to look for Moon. He was sitting under the arcade, his feet against the column and his chair tilted back, smoking. He began as soon as I came within range : —

" Yes, know all about it. You can go there three ways : over the back of a donkey, aboard an Indian canoe, or swim."

" How far is it ? "

" Fifteen miles."

The Titian looked smaller and less important than at any time since my leaving the city of Mexico.

" What do you suggest ? "

" I am not suggesting ; I 'm a passenger."

" You going ? "

" Of course. Think I would leave you here

148

to be murdered by these devils for your watch
key ? "

The picture loomed up once more.

" Then we will take the canoe."

" Next week you will, not now. Listen.
Yesterday was market day ; market day comes
but once a week. There are no canoes on the
beach below us from as far up the lake as Tzintzúntzan, and the fishermen from Zanicho and
towns nearer by refuse to paddle so far."

He threw away his cigar, elongated himself
a foot or more, broke out into a laugh at my
discomfiture, slipped his arm through mine, and
remarked apologetically " that he had sent for
a man and had an idea."

In half an hour the man arrived, and with
him the information that some employees of the
road had recently constructed from two Indian
dug-out canoes a sort of catamaran ; that a deck
had been floored between, a mast stepped, and
a sail rigged thereon. The craft awaited our
pleasure.

Moon's idea oozed out in driblets. Fully developed, it recommended the immediate stock-
ing of the ship with provisions, the hiring of six
Indians with sweep oars, and a start bright and
early on the morrow for Tzintzúntzan ; Moon
to be commodore and hold the tiller ; I to have

149

the captain's stateroom, with free use of the deck.

The morning dawned deliciously cool and bright. Moon followed half an hour later, embodying all the characteristics of the morning and supplementing a few of his own, — another suit of clothes, a cloth cap, and an enormous spyglass.

The clothes were the result of a further exchange of courtesies with a brother engineer, the cap replaced his time-worn broad sombrero, " out of courtesy to the sail," he said, and the spyglass would be useful either as a club of defence, or to pole over shoal places, or in examining the details of the Titian. " The thing might be hung high, and he wanted to see it."

These explanations, however, were cut short by the final preparations for the start, — Moon giving orders in true nautical style, making fast the rudder, calling all hands aft to stow the various baskets and hampers, battening down the trapdoor hatches, and getting everything snug and trim for a voyage of discovery as absurd to him as if entered upon for the finding of the Holy Grail.

Finally all was ready, Moon seized the tiller, and gave the order to cast off. A faint cheer went up from the group of natives on the shore, the wind gave a kindly puff, the six Indians, stripped to their waists, bent to their oars, and the catamaran drifted clear of the gravel beach, and bore away up the lake to Tzintzúntzan.

She was certainly as queer a looking craft as ever trailed a rudder. To be exact, she was about thirty feet long, half as wide, and drew a hand's-breadth of water. Her bow flooring was slightly trimmed to a point; her square stern was protected by a bench a foot wide and high, — forming a sort of open locker under which a man could crawl and escape the sun; her deck was flat, and broken only by the mast, which was well forward, and the rests or giant oarlocks which held the sweeps. The rudder was a curiosity. It was half as long as the boat, and hung over the stern like the pole of an old-fashioned well-sweep. When fulfilling its destiny it had as free charge of the deck as the boom of a fishing smack in a gale of wind. Another peculiarity of the rudder was its independent action. It not only had ideas of its own but followed them. The skipper followed too, after a brief struggle, and walked miles across the deck in humoring its whims. The sail was unique. It was made of a tarpaulin which had seen better days as the fly of a camping tent, and was nailed flat to the short boom which

wandered up and down the mast at will, assisted by half a dozen barrel hoops and the iron
tire of a wheelbarrow. Two trapdoors, cut midway the deck, led into the bowels of the dug-
outs, and proved useful in bailing out leakage
and overwash.

As I was only cabin passenger, and so without responsibility, I stretched my length along
the bench and watched Moon handle the ship.
At first all went smoothly, the commodore
grasped the tiller as cordially as if it had been
the hand of his dearest friend, and the wilful
rudder, lulled to sleep by the outburst, swayed
obediently back and forth. The tarpaulin,
meanwhile, bursting with the pride of its pro-
motion, bent to the breeze in an honest effort
to do its share. Suddenly the wind changed;
the inflated sail lost its head and clung wildly
to the mast, the catamaran careened, Moon
gave a vicious jerk, and the rudder awoke.
Then followed a series of misunderstandings
between the commodore and the thoroughly
aroused well-sweep which enlivened all the
dull passages of the voyage, and introduced
into the general conversation every variety of
imprecation known to me in languages with
which I am familiar, assisted and enlarged by
several dialects understood and appreciated only

152

by the six silent, patient men keeping up their rhythmic movement at the sweeps.

When we reached the first headland on our weather bow the wind freshened to a stiff breeze, and after a brief struggle Moon decided to go about. I saw at a glance that the catamaran held different views, and that it was encouraged and " egged " on, so to speak, by its co-conspirator the rudder.

" You men on the right, stop rowing."

This order was emphasized by an empty bottle thrown from the locker. The three Indians stood motionless.

" Haul that boom," — this to me, sketching with my feet over the stern.

I obeyed with the agility of a man-o'-war's man. The sail flapped wildly, the rudder gave a staggering lurch, and Moon measured his length on the deck !

By the time the commodore had regained his feet he had exhausted his vocabulary. Then with teeth hard set he lashed the rebellious rudder fast to the locker, furled the crestfallen sail, and resigned the boat to the native crew. Five minutes later he was stretched flat on the deck, bubbling over with good humor, and gloating over the contents of the hampers piled up around him.

" That town over your shoulder on the right is Zanicho," he rattled on, pointing with his fork to some adobe huts clustered around a quaint church spire.

" If we had time and a fair wind, I should like to show you the interior. It is exactly as the Jesuits left it three hundred years ago. Away over there on the right is Xarácuaro. You can see from here the ruins of the convent and of half a dozen brown hovels. Nobody there now but fishermen. The only white man in the village is the priest, and I would not wager to his being so all the way through. A little farther along, over that island, if you look close you can see a small town ; it is Igúatzio. There are important Aztec remains about it. A paved roadway leads to the adjoining village, which was built long before the coming of the Span- iards. I do not believe all the marvellous stories told of the Aztec sacrifices, but over the hill yonder is the ruins of the only genuine teo- calli, if there ever was such a thing, in Mexico. I have made a study of these so-called Aztec monuments, and have examined most of the teocallis, or sacrificial mounds, of Montezuma's people without weakening much my unbelief, but I confess this one puzzles me. One day last winter I heard the Indians talking about

154

this mound, and two of us paddled over. It lies in a hollow of the hills back of the town, and is enclosed by a stone wall about one thousand feet long, eight feet high, and four feet wide. The teocalli itself stands in the middle of this quadrangle. It is constructed in the form of a truncated cone about one hundred feet square at the base and nearly as high, built entirely of stone, with an outside stairway winding around its four sides. On one corner of the top are the remains of a small temple. I do not think half a hundred people outside the natives have ever seen it. If it is not a teocalli there is not one in all Mexico. The fact is, no other Aztec mound in Mexico is worthy of the name, — not even Cholula.''

Suddenly a low point, until now hidden by an intervening headland, pushed itself into the lake. Moon reached for his spyglass and adjusted the sliding tube.

'' Do you see those two white specks over that flat shore ?''

'' Perfectly.''

'' And the clump of dark trees surrounding it ?''

'' Yes.''

'' Well, that is Tzintzúntzan. The big speck is what is left of the old Franciscan convent,

155

the clump of trees is the olive orchard, the ancient burial-place of the Aztecs. The little speck is the top of the dome of the convent chapel, beneath which hangs your daub of a Titian.''

XII

TZINTZUNTZAN AND THE TITIAN

THE catamaran rounded the point, floated slowly up to the beach, and anchored on a shoal within a boat's-length of the shore. Strung along the water's edge, with wonder-stricken faces, were gathered half the entire population of Tzintzúntzan. The other half were coming at full speed over the crest of the hill, which partly hid the village itself.

There being but two feet of water, and those wet ones, Moon shot an order in an unknown tongue into the group in front, starting two of them forward, swung himself gracefully over the shoulders of the first, — I clinging to the second, — and we landed dry shod in the midst of as curious a crowd of natives as ever greeted the great Christopher himself.

The splendor which made Tzintzúntzan famous in the days of the good Bishop Quiroga, when its population numbered forty thousand souls, has long since departed. The streets run at right angles, and are divided into squares of apparently equal length, marking a city of some importance in its day. High walls surround each garden and cast grateful shadows. Many of these are broken by great fissures through which can be seen the ruins of abandoned tenements overgrown with weeds and tangled vines. Along the tops of these walls fat melons ripen in the dazzling sun, their leaves and tendrils white with dust, and from the many seams and cracks the cacti flaunt their deep-red blossoms in your face.

We took the path starting from the beach, which widened into a broad road as it crossed the hill, over which could be seen the white spire of the church. This was beaten down by many feet, and marked the daily life of the natives, — from the church to pray, to the shore to fish. With the exception of shaping some crude pottery, they literally do nothing else.

As we advanced along this highway, — Moon carrying his spyglass as an Irishman would his hod over his shoulder, I my umbrella, and the Indians my sketch trap and a basket containing something for the padre, — the wall thickened and grew in height until it ended in a cross wall, behind which stood the ruins of a belfry, the broken bell still clinging to the rotting roof timber. Adjoining this was a crumbling archway without door or hinge.

This forlorn entrance opened into the grounds of the once powerful establishment of San Francisco, closed and in ruins since 1740. Beyond this archway stood another, protected by a heavy double iron grating, which once swung wide to let pass the splendid pageants of the time, now rust-incrusted, and half buried in the ground.

Once inside, the transition was delightful. There was a great garden or orchard planted with olive-trees of enormous size, their tops still alive, and their trunks seamed and gnarled with the storms of three and a half centuries, beneath which lie buried not only the great dignitaries of the Church, but many of the allies and chiefs of Cortez in the times of the Tarascan chieftaincy.

On one side of this orchard is the chapel of the Tercer Order and the Hospital and the convent church, now the *parróquia*. We crossed between the trees and waited outside the convent building at the foot of a flight of stone steps, built along an angle of a projection and leading to the second floor of the building. These steps were crowded with Indians, as was also the passageway within, waiting for an audience with the parish priest, whose apartments were above.

Nothing can adequately describe the dilapidation of this entrance and its surroundings. The steps themselves had been smeared over with mortar to hold them together, the door jambs were leaning and ready to fall, the passageway itself ended in a window which might once have held exquisite panels of stained glass, but which was now open to the elements save where it was choked up with adobe bricks laid loosely in courses. The rooms opening into it were tenantless, and infested with lizards and bats, and the whole place, inside and out, was fast succumbing to a decay which seemed to have reached its limit, and which must soon end in hopeless ruin.

We found the padre seated at a rude table in the darkest corner of a low-ceiled room on the left of the corridor, surrounded by half a dozen Indian women. He was at dinner, and the women were serving him from coarse earthen dishes. When he turned at our intrusion, we saw a short, thickset man, wearing a greasy black frock, a beard a week old, and a smile so treacherous that I involuntarily tapped my inside pocket to make sure of its contents. He arose lazily, gathered upon his coat cuff the few stray crumbs clinging to his lips, and with a searching, cunning air, asked our business.

Moon shifted his spyglass until the large end was well balanced in his hand, and replied obsequiously, "To see the famous picture, holy father. This, my companion, is a distinguished painter from the far East. He has heard of the glory of this great work of the master, of which you are the sacred custodian, and has come these many thousand miles to see it. I hope your reverence will not turn us away."

I saw instantly from his face that he had anticipated this, and that his temper was not improved by Moon's request. I learned afterwards that a canoe had left Pátzcuaro ahead of the catamaran, and that the object of our visit had already been known in Tzintzúntzan some hours before we arrived.

"It is a holy day," replied the padre curtly, "and the sacristy is closed. The picture will not be uncovered."

With this he turned his back upon us and resumed his seat.

I looked at Moon. He was sliding his hand nervously up and down the glass, and clutching its end very much as a man would an Indian club.

"Leave him to me," he whispered from

behind his hand, noticing my disappointment;
"I'll get into that sacristy, if I have to bat
him through the door with this."

In the hamper which Moon had instructed
Griddles, the *chef*, to pack for my comfort the
day before at Morelia, was a small glass vessel,
flat in shape, its contents repressed by a cork
covered with tinfoil. When Moon landed from
the catamaran this vessel was concealed among
some boxes of dulces and fruits from the southern slope, inclosed in a wicker basket, and intrusted to an Indian who now stood within
three feet of the table.

"You are right, holy father," said Moon,
bowing low. "We must respect these holy
days. I have brought your reverence some deli-
cacies, and when the fast is over, you can enjoy them."

Then he piled up in the midst of the rude
earthen platters and clay cups and bowls, —
greasy with the remnants of the meal, — some
bunches of grapes, squares of dulces, and a
small bag of coffee. The flat vessel came last;
this Moon handled lovingly, and with the greatest care, resting it finally against a pulque pot
which the padre had just emptied.

The priest leaned forward, held the flat vessel between his nose and the window, ran his

eyes along the flow line, and glancing at the women turned a dish over it bottom side up.

"When do you return?" he asked.

"To-day, your reverence."

There was a pause, during which the padre buried his face in his hands and Moon played pantomime war dances over the shaved spot on his skull.

"How much will the painter give to the poor of the parish?" said the padre, lifting his head.

After an exposition of the dismal poverty into which the painter was plunged by reason of his calling, it was agreed that upon the payment to the padre of *cinco pesos* in silver — about one pound sterling — the painter might see the picture, when mass was over, the padre adding, —

"There is presently a service. In an hour it will be over; then the sacristan can open the door."

Moon counted out the money on the table, piece by piece. The padre weighed each coin on his palm, bit one of them, and with a satisfied air swept the whole into his pocket.

The tolling of a bell hurried the women from the room. The padre followed slowly, bowing his head upon his breast. Moon and I brought up the rear, passing down the crumbling corridor over the uneven flooring and upturned and

broken tiles and through a low archway until
we reached a gallery overlooking a patio. Here
was a sight one must come to Mexico to see.
Flat on the stone pavements, seated upon mats
woven of green rushes, knelt a score or more
of Indian women, their cheeks hollow from fasting, and their eyes glistening with that strange
glassy look peculiar to half-starved people.
Over their shoulders were twisted black rebozos, and around each head was bound a veritable crown of thorns. In their hands they held
scourges of platted nettles. They had sat here
day and night, without leaving these mats, for
nearly a week.

This terrible ceremony occurs but once a year,
during passion week. The penance lasts eight
days. Each penitent pays a sum of money for
the privilege, and her name and number are then
inscribed upon a sort of tally-board which is
hung on the cloister wall. Upon this are also
kept a record of the punishment. The penitents
provide their zarapes and pillows and the rush
mats upon which to rest their weary bones ;
the priest furnishes everything else, — a little
greasy gruel and the stone pavement.

The padre threaded his way through the
kneeling groups without turning his head to the
right or left. When his footsteps were heard

they repeated their prayers the louder, and one young girl, weak from long fasting, raised her eyes to the priest's pleadingly. His stolid face gave no sign. With downcast eyes she leaned forward, bent low, and kissed the hem of his frock. As she stooped Moon pointed to the marks of the cruel thorns on her temples.

" Shall I maul him a little ?" he whispered, twisting the glass uneasily.

" Wait until we see the Titian," I pleaded.

The cloister led into the chapel. It was bare of even the semblance of a house of worship. But for the altar at one end, and a few lighted candles, it might have passed for the old re- fectory of the convent. We edged our way between the kneeling groups and passed out of a side door into an open court. Moon touched my arm.

" See ! that about measures the poverty of the place," he said. " One coffin for the whole village."

On a rude bier lay a wooden box, narrowed at one end. It was made of white wood, deco- rated on the outside with a rough design in blue and yellow. The bottom was covered with dried leaves, and the imprint of the head and shoulders of the poor fellow who had occupied it a few hours before was still distinct.

"Two underneath, one inside, a mumbled prayer, then he helps to fill the hole and they save the box for the next. A little too narrow for the padre, I am afraid," soliloquized Moon, measuring the width with his eye.

Another tap of the bell, and the Indians straggled out of the church and dispersed, some going to the village, others halting under the great tree trunks, watching us curiously. Indeed, I had before this become aware of an especial espionage over us, which was never relaxed for a single instant. A native would start out from a doorway as soon as we touched the threshold, another would be concealed behind a tree or projecting wall until we passed. Then he would walk away aimlessly, looking back and signalling to another hidden somewhere else. This is not unusual with these natives. They have always resented every overture to part with their picture, and are particularly suspicious of strangers who come from a distance to see it, they worshipping it with a blind idolatry easily understood in their race.

This fear of invasion also extends to their village and church. It has been known for several years that an underground passageway led from a point near the church to the old convent, and in 1855 a party of *savants*, under the direction of Father Aguirre, began to uncover its entrance. No open resistance was made by the natives, but in the silence of the night each stone and shovelful of earth was noiselessly replaced.

A few years later the Bishop of Mexico offered for this picture the sum of twenty thousand pesetas, a sum of money fabulous in their eyes, and which if honestly divided would have made each native richer than an Aztec prince. I do not know whether their religious prejudices influenced them, or whether, remembering the quality of the penance gruel, they dare not trust the padre to divide it, but all the same it was refused. Moon assured me that if the painting ever left its resting place it must go without warning, and be protected by an armed force. It would be certain death to any one to attempt its removal otherwise, and he firmly believed that sooner than see it leave their village the Indians would destroy it.

" Señor, the padre says come to him."

The messenger was a sun-dried, shrivelled Mexican half-breed, with a wicked eye and a beak-like nose. About his head was twisted a red handkerchief, over which was flattened a heavy felt sombrero. He was barefooted, and his trousers were held up by a leather strap.

" Who are you ? " said Moon.

167

" I am the sacristan."

" I thought so. Lead on. A lovely pair of cherubs, are they not ? "

The padre met us at the door. He had sad news for us ; his mortification was extreme. The man who cleaned the sacristy had locked the door that morning and started for Quiroga on a donkey. No one else had a key.

I suggested an immediate chartering of another and somewhat livelier donkey, with instructions to overtake and bring back the man with the key, dead or alive. The padre shrugged his shoulders, and said there was but one donkey in the village, — he was underneath the man with the key. Moon closed one eye and turned the other incredulously on the priest.

" When will the man return ? "

" In three days."

" Your reverence," said the commodore slowly, " do not send for him. It might annoy him to be hurried. We will break in the door and pay for a new lock."

Then followed a series of protests, beginning with the sacrilege of mutilating so sacred a door, and ending with a suggestion from the saffron-colored sacristan that an additional *cinco pesos* would about cover the mutilation, provided every centavo of it was given to the poor of the

parish, and that the further insignificant sum
of five pesetas, if donated to the especial use
of his sun-dried excellency, might induce him
to revive one of his lost arts, and operate on
the lock with a rusty nail.

Moon counted out the money with a sup-
pressed sigh, remarking that he had " always
pitied the poor, but never so much as now."
Then we followed the padre and the sacristan
down the winding steps leading to the cloister,
through the dark corridor, past the entrance to
the chapel, and halted at an arch closed by two
swinging doors. His yellowness fumbled among
some refuse in one corner, picked up a bit of
débris, applied his eyes to an imaginary keyhole, and pushed open a pair of wooden doors
entirely bare of lock, hasp, or latch. They had
doubtless swung loose for half a century! I
had to slip my arm through Moon's and pin his
toes to the pavement to keep him still.

The padre and the half-breed uncovered and
dropped upon their knees. I looked over their
heads into a room about thirty feet long by
twenty wide, with a high ceiling of straight,
square rafters. The floor was paved in great
squares of marble laid diagonally, the walls
were seamed, cracked, and weather-stained.
The only opening other than the door was a

large window, protected on the outside by three
sets of iron gratings, and on the inside by double wooden shutters. The window was without glass. The only articles of furniture visible
were a round table, with curved legs, occupying
the centre of the room, a towel-rack and towel
hung on the wall, and a row of wooden drawers
built like a bureau, completely filling the end
of the room opposite the door. Over this was
hung, or rather fitted, the three sides of a huge
carved frame, showing traces of having once
been gilded, — the space was not high enough to
admit its top member. Inside this frame glowed
the noble picture. I forgot the padre, the oily-
tongued sacristan, and even my friend Moon,
in my wonder, loosened my trap, opened the
stool, and sat down with bated breath to enjoy
it.

My first thought was of its marvellous preservation. More than three hundred years have
elapsed since the great master touched it, and
yet one is deluded into the belief that it was
painted but yesterday, so fresh, pure, and rich
is its color. This is no doubt due to the climate,
and to the clear air circulating through the open
window.

The picture is an Entombment, sixteen feet
long by seven feet high. Surrounding the dead

Christ wrapped in a winding sheet, one end of which is held in the teeth of a disciple, stand the Virgin, Magdalen, Saint John, and nine other figures, all life-size. In the upper left-hand corner is a bit of blue sky, against which is relieved an Italian villa, — the painter's own, a caprice of Titian's often seen in his later works.

The high lights fall upon the arm of the Saviour drooping from the hammock-shaped sheet in which he is carried, and upon the head-covering of the Virgin bending over him. A secondary light is found in the patch of blue sky. To the right and behind the group of disciples the shadows are intensely dark, relieving the rich tones of the browns and blues in the draperies, and the flesh tones for which the painter is famous. The exquisite drawing of each figure, the gradation of light and shade, the marvellous composition, the relief and modelling of the Christ, the low but luminous tones in which it is painted, the superb harmony of these tones, all pronounce it the work of a master.

The questions naturally arise, Is it by Titian? and if so, How came it here in an Indian village in the centre of Mexico, and why has it been lost all these years to the art world? To the first I answer, If not by Titian, who then of his

171

time could paint it ? The second is easier : Until the railroads of the last few years opened up the country, Mexico's isolation was complete.

A slight résumé of the history of its surroundings may shed some light on these questions. After the ruin wrought in Michoacan in the early part of the sixteenth century by the evil acts of Niño de Guzman, — the president of the first Audencia, — terminating in the burning of the Tarascan chief Sinzicha, the people, maddened with terror, fled to the mountains around Tzintzúntzan and refused to return to their homes. To remedy these evils, the Emperor Charles V. selected the members of the second Audencia from among the wisest and best men of Spain. One of these was an intimate friend of the emperor, an eminent lawyer, the Licenciado Vasco de Quiroga. Being come to Mexico, Don Vasco, in the year 1533, visited the depopulated towns, and with admirable patience, gentleness, and love, prevailed on the terror-stricken Indians to have faith in him and return to their homes.[1]

The bishopric of Michoacan was then founded, and this mitre was offered to Quiroga, though he was then a layman. Thereupon Quiroga took holy orders, and having been raised quickly through the successive grades of the priesthood,

[1] Janvier's *Mexican Guide*.

was consecrated a bishop and took possession of his see in the church of San Francisco in Tzintzúntzan August 22, 1538. He was then sixty-eight years old. As bishop, he completed the conquest through love that he had begun while yet a layman. He established schools of letters and the arts; introduced manufactures of copper and other metals; imported from Spain cattle and seeds for acclimatization; founded hospitals, and established the first university of New Spain, that of San Nicholas, now in Morelia.

When Philip II. ascended the throne the good deeds of the holy bishop had reached his ears, and the power and growth of his see had deeply touched the heart of the devout monarch, — awakening in his mind a profound interest in the welfare of the church at Tzintzúntzan and Pátzcuaro. During this period the royal palaces at Madrid were filled with the finest pictures of Titian, and the royal family of Spain formed the subjects of his best portraits. The Emperor Charles V. had been and was then one of the master's most liberal patrons. He had made him a count, heaped upon him distinguished honors, and had been visited by him twice at Augsburg and once at Bologna, where he painted his portrait. It is even claimed by some biographers that by special invitation of his royal patron Titian visited Spain about the year 1550, and was entertained with great splendor at the court. Moreover, it is well known that he was granted a pension, and that this was kept up by Philip until the painter's death.

Remembering the dates at which these events took place; the fanatical zeal of Philip, and his interest in the distant church, redeemed and made glorious by Quiroga, the friend and *protégé* of his royal predecessor; the possible presence of Titian at the court at the time, certainly the influence of his masterpieces, together with the fact that the subject of this picture was a favorite one with him, notably the Entombment in Venice and the *replica* at the Louvre, it is quite within the range of probability that Philip either ordered this especial picture from the master himself, or selected it from the royal collection.

It is quite improbable, in view of the above facts, that the royal donor would have sent the work of an inferior painter, representing it to be by Titian, or a copy by one of his pupils.

Another distinguishing feature, and by far the most conclusive, is its handling. Without strong contrasting tones of color, Titian worked out a peculiar golden mellow tone, — which of

itself exercises a magical charm, — and divided
it into innumerable small but significant shades,
producing thereby a most complete illusion of
life. This Titianesque quality is particularly
marked in the nude body of the Christ, the flesh
appearing to glow with a hidden light.

Moon's criticisms were thoroughly characteristic. He hoped I was satisfied. Did I want to
see both sides of it ? If I did, he would push out
the rear wall. Would the spyglass be of any
use, etc. I waved him away, opened my easel,
and began a hurried memorandum of the interior, and a rough outline of the position of the
figures on the canvas. When his retreating
footsteps echoed down the corridor, I closed the
doors gently behind him and resumed my work.
The picture absorbed me. I wanted to be shut
up alone with it.

A sense of a sort of temporary ownership
comes over one when left alone in a room containing some priceless treasure or thing of beauty
not his own. It is a selfish pleasure which is undisturbed, and which you do not care to share
with another. For the time being you monopolize
it, and it is as really your own as if you had the
bill of sale in your pocket. I deluded myself with
this fancy, and began examining more closely
the iron gratings of the window and the manner

of fastening them to the masonry, wondering whether they would always be secure. I inspected all the rude ornaments on the front of the drawers of the wide, low bureau which stood immediately beneath the picture ; opened one of them a few inches and discovered a bundle of vestments, dust-covered and spattered with candle grease. Lifting myself up I noted the carving of the huge frame, and followed the lines of the old gilding into its dust-begrimed channels ; and to make a closer study of the texture of the canvas and the handling of the pigments, I mounted the bureau itself and walked the length of the painting, applying my pocket magnifying glass to the varnished surface. When I stood upright the drooping figure of the Christ reached nearly to the level of my eye. Looking closer, I found the over-glaze to be rich and singularly transparent, and after a careful scrutiny fancied I could separate into distinct tones the peculiar mosaic of color in which most of all lies the secret of Titian's flesh. In the eagerness of my search I unconsciously bent forward and laid my hand upon the Christ.

"*Cuidado! Estrangero, es muerte!*" (Beware! Stranger, it is death!) came a quick, angry voice in my rear.

I started back with my heart in my mouth. Behind me, inside the doors, stood two Indians. One advanced threateningly, the other rushed out shouting for the padre. In an instant the room was crowded with natives clamoring wildly, and pointing at me with angry looks and gestures. The padre arrived breathless, followed by Moon, who had forced his way through the throng, his big frame towering above the others.

During the hubbub I kept my place on the bureau, undecided what to do.

"You have put your foot in it!" said Moon to me in English, in a tone of voice new to me from him. "Do exactly what I tell you, and perhaps we may get away from here with a whole skin. Turn your face to the picture." I did so. "Now come down from that old clothes-press backwards, get down on your knees, and bow three times, you lunatic."

I had sense enough left to do this reverently, and with some show of ceremony.

Then, without moving a muscle of his face, and with the deepest earnestness, Moon turned to the padre and said, —

"The distinguished painter is a true believer, holy father. His hand had lost its cunning and he could no longer paint. He was told in a dream to journey to this place, where he would find his sacred treasure, upon touching which his hand would regain its power. See ! Here is the proof.''

The padre examined the sketch resting upon my easel, and, without taking his eye from Moon, repeated the miracle to the Indians in their own tongue. The change in their demeanor was instantaneous. The noise ceased ; a silence fell upon the group and they crowded about the drawing, wonderstruck. Moon bowed low to the padre, caught up the standing easel, threw my trap over his shoulder, pushed me ahead of him ; an opening was made, — the people standing back humbly, — and we passed through the crowd and out into the sunlight.

Once clear of the church he led the way straight to the catamaran, hoisted the sail, manned the sweeps, swung the rudder clear of the shoal, and headed for Pátzcuaro. When everything was snug and trim for the voyage home, and the catamaran had drifted slowly out into the deep water of the lake, the commodore lounged down the deck, laid his hand upon my shoulder, and said, half reprovingly, —

'' Well, you beat the devil.''

When we pushed off from Tzintzúntzan, the afternoon sun was glorifying our end of the

178

universe, and in our delirium we fancied we had
but to spread our one wing to reach bed and
board, fifteen miles distant, before the rosy
twilight could fade into velvet blue. But the
wind was contrary. It was worse — it was ma-
licious. It blew south, then north, and then
took a flying turn all around the four points
of the compass, and finally settled down to a
steady freshness dead ahead. For hours at a
time low points of land and high hills guarded
by sentinel trees anchored themselves off our
weather bow as if loath to part from us, and
remained immovable until an extra spurt at the
sweeps drove them into the darkness. To return
was hazardous, to drift ashore dangerous, to
advance almost impossible. As the night wore
on the wind grew tired of frolicking and went
careering over the mountains behind us. Then
the lake grew still, and the sweeps gained upon
the landscape and point after point floated off
mysteriously and disappeared in the gloom.

All night we lay on the deck, looking up at
the stars and listening to the steady plashing
of the sweeps, pitying the poor fellows at their
task and lending a hand now and then to give
them a breathing spell. The thin crescent of
the new moon, which had glowed into life as
the color left the evening sky, looked at us

wonderingly for a while, then concluding that we intended making a night of it, dropped down behind the hills of Zanicho and went to bed. Her namesake wrapped his own coat about me, protesting that the night air was bad for foreigners, threw one end of the ragged tarpaulin over his own shoulders, tucked a hamper under his head, and spent the night moralizing over the deliberate cruelty of my desertion in the morning.

It was a long and dreary voyage. The provender was exhausted. There was not on board a crumb large enough to feed a fly. Between the padre, the six Indians, and ourselves every fig, dulce, bone, crust, and drop had disappeared.

When the first streak of light illumined the sky we found ourselves near enough to Pátzcuaro to follow the outline of the hills around the town and locate the little huts close to the shore. When the dawn broke clear we were pushing aside the tall grass near the beach, and the wild fowl, startled from their haunts, were whirling around our heads.

The barking of a dog aroused the inmates of a cabin near the water's edge, and half an hour later Moon was pounding coffee in a bag and I devilling the legs of a turkey over a charcoal brazier, — the inmates had devoured all but the drumsticks the night before. We were grateful that he was not a cripple. While the savory smell of the toasted *cacone*, mingled with the aroma of boiling coffee, filled the room, Moon set two plates, cut some great slices of bread from a loaf which he held between his knees, and divided equally the remnants of the frugal meal. Two anatomical specimens picked clean and white and two empty plates told the story of our appetites.

" At eight o'clock, *caro mio*, the train returns to the East. Do you still insist on being barbarous enough to leave me ? What have I done to you that you should treat me thus ?"

I pleaded my necessities. I had reached the end of my journey. My task was completed ; henceforth my face must be set towards the rising sun. Would he return as far with me as Zacatécas, or even to the city of Mexico ?

No, he expected a despatch from his chief. He would stay at Pátzcuaro.

I expected this. It was always his chief. No human being had ever seen him ; no messenger had ever brought news of his arrival ; no employee had ever explained his delay. In none of the cities through which we had travelled had Moon ever spent five minutes in looking him up, or ten seconds in regretting his absence.

A WHITE UMBRELLA IN MEXICO

When my traps were aboard, and the breezy, happy-hearted fellow had wrung my hand for the twentieth time, I said to him, —

" Moon, one thing before we part. Have you ever seen your chief for a single instant since we left Toluca ?"

He looked at me quizzically, closed his left eye, — a habit with him when anything pleased him greatly, — and replied, —

" A dozen times."

" Where ?" I asked doubtingly.

" When I shave."

IN OTHER LANDS

UNDER THE MINARETS

IT was a small, not over-clean, and much crumpled card.

It was held very near my nose, and above the heads of a struggling, snarling pack of Turks, Armenians, Greeks, and Jews, all yelling at the tops of their voices, and all held at bay by a protecting rail in the station and two befezzed officers attached to the custom-house of his Serene Highness. It bore this inscription: —

ISAAC ISAACS,

Dragoman and Interpreter,

Constantinople.

Beyond this seething mass of Orientals was seen an open door, and through this only the sunlight, a patch of green grass, and the glimpse of a minaret against the blue.

Yes; one thing more — the card.

The owner carried it aloft, like a flag of truce. He had escaped the tax-gathering section of the

Sublime Porte by dodging under the guarded rail, and with fez to earth was now pressing its oblong proportions within an inch of my eyeglasses.

"Do you speak English ? "

"Ev'ting: Yerman, Franche, Grek, Tearkish — all ! "

"Take this sketch trap, and get me a carriage."

The fez righted itself, and I looked into the face of a swarthy, dark-bearded mongrel, with a tobacco-colored complexion and a watery eye. He was gasping for breath and reeking with perspiration, the back of his hand serving as sponge.

I handed him my check, — through baggage Orient Express, two days from Vienna, — stepped into the half-parched garden, and drank in my first full breath of Eastern air.

Within the garden — an oasis, barely kept alive by periodical sprinkling — lounged a few railroad officials hugging scant shadows, and one lone Turk dispensing cooling drinks beneath a huge umbrella.

Outside the garden's protecting fence wandered half the lost tribes of the earth. Some staggered under huge casks of wine swung on poles ; some bent under cases as large as pianos ;

some were hawking bread, Turkish sweets, grapes, and sugared figs; some were peddling clothes, some sandals, some water-jars : each splitting the air with a combination of shouts and cries that would have done justice to a travelling menagerie two hours late for breakfast. In and out this motley mob slouched the dogs, — in the middle of the street, under the benches, in everybody's way and under everybody's feet : everywhere dogs, dogs, dogs !

Beyond this babel straggled a low building attached to the station. Above rose a ragged hill crowned by a shimmering wall of dazzling white, topped with rounded dome and slender minarets. Over all was the beautiful sky of the East, the joy and despair of every brush from the earliest times down to my own.

Ever since the days of the Arabian Nights — my days — the days of Haroun al Raschid, of the big jars with the forty scalded thieves and the beautiful Fatima with the almond-shaped eyes, I have dreamed of the Orient and its palaces of marble. And so, when Baron de Hirsch had brought the home of the Caliphs within two days' journey of the domes of San Marco, I threw some extra canvases into a trunk, tucked a passport into my inside pocket, shouldered my sketch trap, and bought a second-class ticket for Constantinople.

I had only one object, to paint.

My comrades at Florian's — that most delightful of caffès on the Piazza — when they heard that I was about to exchange the cool canals of my beloved Venice for the dusty highways of the unspeakable Turk, condemned my departure as quixotic. The fleas would devour me ; the beggars (all bandits) steal my last franc ; and the government lock me up the very first moment I loosened my sketch trap.

But Isaac Isaacs, the dragoman, is standing obsequiously with fez in hand, two little rivulets of well-earned sweat coursing down each cheek.

" Ze baggages ees complet, effendi."

Isaac crawled upon the box, the driver, a bare-legged Turk with fez and stomach sash, drove his heel into the haunches of the near horse, once, no doubt, the pride of the desert, and we whirled away in a cloud of dust.

" I don't see my trunk, Isaac."

" Not presently, effendi. It now arrives immediatamente at the dogane. Trust me ! "

Five minutes more, and we alighted at the custom-house.

" This way, effendi."

For the benefit of those unfamiliar with the liquid language of the Orient, I will say that effendi means master, and that it is never applied except to some distinguished person, — one who has, or is expected to have, the sum of half a piastre about his person.

Isaac presented the check — a scrap of paper — to another befezzed official, and the next moment ushered me into a small room on the ground floor, furnished with a divan, a tray with coffee and cigarettes, and an overfed, cross-legged Turk. There was also a secretary, curled up somewhere in a corner, scratching away with a pen.

I salaamed to the Turk, detailed into the secretary's ear an account of my birth and ancestry, my several occupations and ambitions, my early life at home, my past life in Venice, and my present intentions in Constantinople. I then opened my passport, sketch-book, and trap, and delivered up the key of my trunk.

The secretary undid his legs, stamped upon my official passport a monogram of authority looking more like the image of a fish-worm petrified in the last agonies of death than any written sign with which I was familiar, and clapped his hands in a perfectly natural Aladdin sort of way. A *genie* in the shape of a Nubian, immeasurably black, moved from behind a curtain, and in five minutes my trunk holding the extra canvases, with a great white cross of peace chalked upon its face, was strapped to the carriage, and we on our way to the Royal.

As I said before, I had come to Constantinople to paint. Not to study its exquisite palaces and mosques; its marvellous stuffs; its romantic history; its religion, the most profound and impressive; its commerce, industries, and customs; but simply to paint. To revel in color; to sit for hours following with reverent pencil the details of an architecture unrivalled on the globe; to watch the sun scale the hills of Scutari, and shatter its lances against the fairy minarets of Stamboul; to catch the swing and plash of the rowers rounding their caïques by the bridge of Galata; to wander through bazaar, plaza, and market, dotting down splashes of robe, turban, and sash; to rest for hours in cool tiled mosques, with the silence of the infinite about me; to steep my soul in a splendor which in its very decay is sublime; and to study a people whose rags are symphonies of color, whose traditions and records the sweetest poems of modern times. If you are content with only this, then come with me to the patio of the Mosque Bayazid — the Pigeon Mosque.

Isaac Isaacs, dragoman, stands at its door, with one hand over his heart, the other raised aloft, invoking the condemnation of the gods if he lies. In his earnestness he is pushing back his fez, disclosing an ugly old scar in his wrinkled, leathery forehead, a sabre cut, he tells me, in a burst of confidence, won in the last row with Russia. His black beard is shaking like a goat's, while his hands, with upturned palms and thumbs, touch his shoulders with the old wavy motion common to his race. Standing now in the shadow of the archway, he insists that no unbeliever is ever permitted to make pictures in the patio, where flows the sacred fountain, and where the priests and faithful wash their feet before entering the holy temple.

I had heard something like this before. The idlers at Florian's had all said so ; an intelligent Greek merchant whom I met on the train had been sure of it ; and even the clerk of the Royal shrugged his shoulders and thought I had better not.

All this time — Isaac still invoking new gods — I was gazing into the most beautiful patio along the Golden Horn, feasting my eyes on columns of verd antique supporting arches light as rainbows.

Crossing the threshold, I dropped my trap

191

behind a protecting column, and ran my eye around the Moorish square. The sun blazed down on glistening marbles; gnarled old cedars twisted themselves upward against the sky; flocks of pigeons whirled and swooped and fell in showers on cornice, roof, and dome; and tall minarets, like shafts of light, shot up into the blue. Scattered over the uneven pavement, patched with strips and squares of shadows, lounged groups of priests in bewildering robes of mauve, corn-yellow, white, and sea-green, while back beneath the cool arches bunches of natives listlessly pursued their several avocations.

It was a sight that brought the blood with a rush to my cheek. Here at last was the East, the land of my dreams! That swarthy Mussulman at his little square table mending seals; that fellow next him selling herbs, sprawled out on the marble floor, too lazy to crawl away from the slant of the sunshine slipping through the ragged awning; and that young Turk in frayed and soiled embroidered jacket, holding up strings of beads to the priests passing in and out, —had I not seen them over and over again?

And the old public scribe with the gray beard and white turban, writing letters, the motionless veiled figures squatting around him, was he not Baba Mustapha, and the soft-eyed girl

ALONG THE GOLDEN HORN.

whispering into his ear, none other than Morgiana, "fair as the meridian sun"?

Was I to devour all this with my eyes, and fill my soul with its beauty, and take nothing away? My mind was made up the moment I looked into the old scribe's face. Once get the confidence of this secret repository of half the love-making and intrigue in Stamboul, and I was safe.

"Isaac!"

"Yes, effendi."

"Do you know the scribe?"

Isaac advanced a step, scrutinized the old patriarch for a moment, and replied, —

"Effendi, pardonnez, he the one only man in Stamboul I not know."

This time, I noticed, he omitted the invocation to the gods.

"Then I 'll present you."

I waited until the scribe looked up and caught my eye. Then I bowed my head reverently, and gave him the Turkish salute. It is a most respectful salutation. You stoop to the ground, pick up an imaginary handful of dust, press it to your heart, lips, and forehead, in token of your sincerity and esteem, and then scatter it to the four winds of heaven. Rapidly done, it looks like brushing off a fly.

The old scribe arose with the dignity of King Solomon — I am quite sure he looked like him — and offered me his own straw-thatched stool. I accepted it gravely, and opened my cigarette case.

He unseated a client, dismissed his business for the day, and sat down beside me. Then, Isaac interpreting, I turned my sketch-book leaf by leaf, showing bits of Venice, and in the back of the book some tall minarets of an old mosque caught on my way through Bulgaria.

It was curious to watch his face as the drago-man located for him the several scraps and blots, and explained their meaning. He evidently had never seen their like before. When he came to the minaret, his eye brightened, and pointing upward to the one above our heads, he drew an imaginary outline with his hand, and pointed to me. I nodded my head. At this he looked grave, and I forthwith sent Isaac for coffee, and lighted another cigarette. Before the cups were emptied I had formally and with great cere-mony asked and received permission to paint the most sacred patio, Isaac protesting all the time in high dudgeon as he unbuckled my trap, that the scribe was a common pauper, earning but a spoonful of copper coin in a day, with no more right to grant me a permit than the flea-bitten beggar at the gate. It was evident that Isaac had not come to Constantinople to paint.

Half an hour later the arches were sketched in, the pillars and roof line complete, and I was rapidly nearing that part of my work in which the pencil is exchanged for the palette, when the shrill voice of the muezzin calling the faithful to prayer sounded above my head. I could see his little white dot of a turban bobbing away high above me on the minaret, his blue robe waving in the soft air.

In an instant priests, seal-maker, herb doctor, and pedler, crowded about the fountain, washed their faces and feet, and moved silently and reverently into the mosque. Soon the patio was deserted by all except Isaac, the pigeons, and the scribe, — the kindly old scribe, — who remained glued to his seat, lost in wonder.

Another hour, and the worshippers came straggling back, resuming their several avocations. Last of all came the priests, in groups of eight or ten, flashing masses of color as they stepped out of the cool arches into the blinding sunlight. They approached my easel with that easy rhythmic movement, so gracefully accentuated by their flowing robes, stopped short, and silently grouped themselves about me. I had now the creamy white of the minaret sharp

195

against the blue, and the entrance of the mosque in clear relief.

For an instant there was a hurried consultation. Then a beardless young priest courteously but firmly expounded to Isaac some of the fundamental doctrines of the Mohammedan faith, —this one in particular: "Thou shalt not paint."

Before I could call to Isaac, I felt a hand caress my shoulder, and raised my head. The scribe, with faded robe gathered about him, stood gazing into the face of the speaker. I held my breath, wondering whether, after all, I had left San Marco in vain. Isaac remained mute, a half-triumphant "I told you so" expression lighting up his face.

Then the old scribe waved Isaac aside, and, drawing himself to his full height, his long beard blending with his white robe, answered in his stead. "I have given my word to the Frank. He is not a giaour, but a true Moslem, a holy man, who loves our temple. I have broken bread with him. He is my friend, bone of my bone, blood of my blood. You cannot drive him away."

After that, painting about Constantinople became quite easy. Perhaps the priests told it to their fellow priests, who spread it abroad among the faithful in the mosques; perhaps the gossips around the patio took it up, or the good scribe whispered it into the veiled ear of his next fair client, and so gave it wings. How it happened, I know not; but from that day my white umbrella became a banner of peace, and my open sketch-book a passport to everybody's courtesy and everybody's good will.

Let me remind those who may have forgotten it that there is really no such place as Constantinople. There is, of course, the old Turkish city of Stamboul, with all the great mosques: the mosque of the Six Minarets, the Sultana Valedé, Soliman, and some hundred others, and where, moreover, one finds the great bazaar — twelve miles of arcaded streets in a tangle — the cafés, drug-markets, fish-markets, spice-markets, vile-smelling, dirt-choked alleys and baths.

Then there is the European city of Pera, up a hill, — a long way up, — with its modern tramway below, and the ancient tower of the Genoise crowning the top. Pera, rebuilt since the fire, with its new hotels and foreign embassies, its modern shops filled with machine-made Oriental embroideries, and its more modern streets flanked by the everlasting four-story house with the flat roof and balcony, and the same old cast-iron railings and half-dead potted plants. Pera, the commonplace, except, perhaps, for one delightfully picturesque old cemetery with its curious headstones and dismal cypresses which could not be burned, and so could not be rebuilt and ruined.

And last, across the Bosporus, is Scutari, only ten minutes by ferry-boat. Scutari-in-Asia, with mosques, archways, palaces, seraglios, fruit-markets, Arab horses, priests, eunuchs with bevies of houris out for an airing, gay awnings, silks in festoons from shop doors, streets crowded with carnival-like people wearing every color under the sun, Bedouins on horseback riding rapidly through narrow streets, tons and tons of grapes piled up in baskets, soldiers in fez and brown linen suits, — everything that is foreign and un-European, and out of the common world. A bewildering, overwhelming, intoxicating sight to a man who has travelled one half the world over to find the picturesque, and who suddenly comes upon all there is in the other half, crammed into one compact mass a mile square.

Isaac never quite understands why I go about absorbed in these things, and why I ignore the regulation sights, — the mosque with the Persian tiles, three miles away and a carriage;

the treasury at Seraglio Point, opened only by permit from the Grand Vizier (price £2); the dancing dervishes at Pera; the howling dervishes at Scutari; and the identical spot where Leander plunged into the sea.

I finally compromised with Isaac on the dervishes. We had spent the morning at Scutari, where I had been painting an old mosque. It was howling-dervish day, — it comes but once a week, the howl beginning at three P. M. precisely, — and to satisfy Isaac I had left the sunshine for an hour to watch their curious service.

I had, it is proper to state, wrung a confession that morning from Isaac which had so humiliated him that he had suggested the dervishes to divert my attention. A dragoman of the opposition, a veritable son of Abraham, had betrayed him. He had bitten his thumb at him, not literally but figuratively, and this in very decent English — no, the reverse. He had charged him with fraud. He had said that his name was not Isaac Isaacs, but Yapouly — Dreco Yapouly; that he was not an honest Jew, but a dog of a Turk, who had stolen honest Isaac's name when he died. Yes, robbed him, ghoul, gravedigger, beast! He with a scar on his forehead, where he had been branded for theft! And here the opposition dragoman snatched Isaac's fez from his head, and ground it into the dirt with his heel.

After a gendarme had taken this very disagreeable opposition dragoman away, Isaac had confessed. So many Englishmen, Frenchmen, Americans, he said, had wanted Mr. Isaacs that he had concluded that it was cruel not to accommodate them. Of what use, estimable effendi, was a dead Jew? How infinitely better a live Turk! So one day, when hanging over the rail at the station, an Englishman had arrived holding the deceased Isaac's card in his hand, and since that time Yapouly had been Isaac Isaacs to the stranger and the wayfaring man. "See, effendi, here the Angleeshman card."

It was the same the rascal had pressed into my own face!

Thus it was that Dreco Yapouly Isaacs — I will no longer lend myself to his villanous deception — preceded me this day up a steep hill paved with boulders, entered the low door of the *tekkè* (house) of the dervishes, and motioned me to a seat in a small open court sheltered by an arbor covered with vines.

In the centre was a well, flagged by a great stone, and on this rested a high, narrow-necked silver pitcher of perfect Oriental shape used by the priests in their ablutions. At the door of the sacred room stood a stalwart Nubian dressed in pure white — ten times as black by contrast.

Five francs, and we passed the hanging curtain covering the entrance, and stepped inside a square, low-ceiled room hung with tambourines, cymbals, arms, and banners, and surrounded on three sides by an aisle.

The howlers — there were at least a dozen — were standing in a straight row on the floor, like a class at school, facing their master, an old, long-bearded priest squatting on a mat before the altar.

As we entered, they were wagging their heads in unison, keeping time to a chant monotoned by the old priest. They were of all ages; fat and lean, smooth-shaven and bearded; some in rich garments, others in more sombre and cheaper stuffs.

One face cut itself into my memory, — that of a handsome, clear-skinned young man, with deep, intense eyes and a sinewy, graceful body. On one of his delicate, lady-white hands was a large turquoise ring. Yapouly whispered to me that he was the son of the high priest, and would succeed his father when the old man died.

The chant continued, rising in volume and intensity, and a Nubian in white handed each man a black skull-cap. These they drew tightly over their perspiring heads.

The movement, which had begun with the slow rolling of their heads, now extended to their bodies. They writhed and twisted as if in agony, — a row of black-capped felons suspended from unseen ropes.

Suddenly there darted out upon the mats a boy scarce ten years of age, spinning like a top, his skirts level with his hands.

The chant broke into a wail, the audience joining in. The howls were deafening. The priest rose from the mats by the altar, slowly waved his hands, and began moving around the room, the worshippers reaching forward and kissing the hem of his robe. As he passed, each dervish stepped one pace forward, and handed his outer robe to the Nubian, who piled them on the floor in front of the altar.

The twelve were now rocking their heads in a wild frenzy, groaning in long subdued moans, ending in a peculiar "hough," like the sound of a dozen distant locomotives tugging up a steep grade.

"Allah, hou! Allah, hou! Allah, hou!" — the last word expelled with a jerk. Their eyes were starting from their heads, their parched tongues hanging out, the sweat pouring from their faces. The young priest was livid, with eyes closed, — his body swaying uneasily.

A dozen little children were here handed over the rail to the Nubian, who took them in his arms and laid them in a row with their faces flattened to the mats. The old priest advanced within a step of the first child, his lips moving in prayer, and stretched his arms above the motionless line of fat, chubby little bodies.

Yapouly Isaacs leaned over and whispered, "See, now he bless them."

I raised myself on my feet, to see the better. The Nubian held out his hand to the old priest, who balanced himself for a moment, stepped firmly upon the first child, his bare feet sinking into its soft, yielding flesh, and then walked deliberately across the row of prostrate children. As he passed, each little tot raised its head, watched until the last child had been trampled upon, then sprang up, kissed the old priest's robe, and ran laughing from the room.

The sight now was sickening; the dervishes were in the last stages of exhausted frenzy. The once handsome young priest was ghastly, frothing at the mouth, only the whites of his eyes visible, — his voice was thick, his breath almost gone. The others were drooping, with knees bent, hardly able to stand.

Suddenly the priest turned his back, prostrated himself before the altar, and prayed silently. The whirling child sank to the ground. The line of dervishes grew still, tottered along the floor, clutched at the hanging curtain, and staggered into the sunlight.

I forced my way along the closely packed aisle, and rushed into the open air. The sight that met my eye stunned me ; my breath stopped short. In the midst of the court stood the Nubian serving coffee, the howlers crowding about him, clamoring for cups, and panting for breath like a team of athletes in from a foot-race. I looked for my young priest with the turquoise ring. He was sitting on a bench, rolling a cigarette, his face wreathed with smiles !

And yet the Mohammedan priest, despite his fanaticism, is really a most delightful companion. His tastes are refined, his garments spotless, his manners easy and graceful, and his whole bearing distinguished by a repose that is superb, — the repose of unlimited idleness dignified by unquestioned religious authority.

I remember one in particular who spent a morning with me, — a noble old patriarch, dressed in a delicate eggshell-colored robe that floated about his feet as he walked, an under-garment of mauve, with waist sash of pale blue, and a snowdrift of silk on his head. For four broiling hours, with only such shade as a half-withered plane-tree could afford, did this majestic old fellow, with slippers tucked under him, sit and drink in every movement of my brush. When I had finished, he arose, saluted me after the manner of his race, and pointing first to the sketch, and then to the glistening mosque, said, in the softest of voices, —

" Good dragoman, tell your master I have for him a very great respect. He has opened my eyes to many beautiful things. I am sure he is a most learned man," and passed on with the dignity and composure of a Doge.

Everywhere else did I find this same spontaneous, generous courtesy and kindly good-humor. Only once was I rebuffed. It was in the open plaza of the Valedé. I had been watching the shifting scene, following eagerly the little dabs of color hurrying over the heated pavement, when my eye fell upon a cobbler but a few yards off, pegging away at an upturned shoe. When my restless pencil had fastened his fez upon his head, and linked his body to his three-legged stool, a laugh broke out among the bystanders crowded about me, one jovial old Turk calling out to the unconscious model. In a moment he was on his feet, forcing his way through the throng behind me. Then a hand clutched my shoulder, and the next instant a wet leather sole was thrust forward and ground into my paper, spoiling the sketch.

It took five minutes of my most subtle Oriental diplomacy, sweetened with several cups of the choicest Turkish coffee, to convince this indignant shoemaker that I meant no offence. When I had succeeded, he was so profuse in his apologies that I had to smoke a chibouque with him, at his expense, to restore his equanimity.

And yet, under all the courtesy and good-nature I found everywhere, I could not help noticing that a certain disquiet and nervous fear permeated all classes, — priests and people alike. The government's extreme poverty and constant watchfulness are two things the inhabitant never forgets, — one concerns his taxes, the other his liberty. This fear is so great that many public topics worn threadbare by most Europeans are never whispered by a Turk to his most intimate friend. Even my dear friend and confidential adviser, Mr. Yapouly, finds now and then a subject upon which he is silent. One day I asked him who had

been suspected of murdering the predecessor of
the present Sultan, and why it had been thought
necessary to remove that luxurious son of the
Prophet. It was an idle question on my part,
and one I supposed anybody in Constantinople
could answer, especially so learned and versatile a dragoman as Mr. Yapouly. To my surprise he made no reply ; we were in Pera at the
time, he preceding me with the trap. When
we reached the long cemetery, he stopped,
looked carefully over the low wall, as if fearing
the very graves, and then said, in his broken
conglomerate, too shattered to reproduce here :

"Effendi, you must not ask such questions.
Everybody is a spy, — the man asleep on the
sofa in the hotel, the waiter behind your chair,
the barber who shaves you. Some night your
bed will be empty. Nobody ever asks such
questions in Constantinople."

Nor is this unrest confined to the people. I
noticed the same anxious look on the Sultan's
face the day of the *salemlik*, the day he drives
publicly to the little mosque to pray, the mosque
outside the palace gates. His face was like that
of the acrobat riding bareback at the circus hoop
— glad to be through.

But I am in Constantinople to paint, not to
moralize, and these glimpses of the treacherous

deadly stream that flows beneath Turkish
life are not to my liking. I want only the gay
flowers above its banks and the soft summer
air on my cheek, the tall grasses waving in the
sunlight, and the glow and radiance of it all.
So, if you please, we will go back to my mosque,
and my delightful old priests, and the Greek
who sells me grapes and weighs them in a pair
of teetering scales, and my caïque with the pew
cushion over the bottom, and the big caïkjis,
with the chest of a Hercules and the legs of
a satyr, who rows my Oriental gondola, and
all the beautiful patches of color, fretted arch,
and slender column that make life enchanting in this lotus-eating land ; and even to
Mr. Yapouly, Mr. Dreco Yapouly, who tells
me he has reformed, and will never lie more,
"so help him," — Mr. Dreco Isaacs Yapouly,
who has lately ceased his unanswered appeals
to the gods, and who has left off all his evil
ways.

But then I remember that I cannot go back
to my old life now, for the summer is ended.
Last night there was a great storm of wind and
a deluge of rain, the first for four months. All
the gold-dust has been washed from the trees
and the grasses. The plaza of the Valedé is
scoured clean. The little waves around the

Galata no longer lap their tongues indolently about the soggy, rotten floats, but snap angrily in the bleak wind. The doors of the mosques are closed, and outside, in the early morning, groups of natives are huddled over charcoal pans. The winter is creeping on apace, and I must be gone. Besides, they are waiting for me at Florian's on the Piazza in my beloved Venice; those scoffers with their cerise and Chianti and *grandi* of Munich beer. Waiting, not to mock, but to kotow, to bend the ear and genuflect, now that my portfolio is bursting, and to say, " Come, let us see your stuff ! " and " How the devil did you get away with so much ? "

So one morning I tell Isaac to pack my trap, and this time to slip it inside its leather travelling-case, and to get me a " hamal," a human burro — an Armenian, perhaps — who will toss my trunk, with the extra canvases now all filled, upon his back, and never break trot until he dumps it at the station two miles away.

I instantly detect, in spite of our close intimacy, an expression of relief wrinkling Mr. Yapouly's tobacco-colored countenance. He sighs his regrets, but with a lightness that shows his heart is not in them. He has been but a " hamal " himself, he thinks, lugging the trap about in the heat, and sitting for hours doing nothing — absolutely nothing. And I have bought so little in the bazaars, and his commissions are so small! But then, as he reflects, is he not the dragoman of dragomans, and might not future wayfarers be my intimate friends and his special prey? So he becomes doubly solicitous as the time draws near. Would effendi allow him to place a few pounds of grapes in the compartment, the road to Philippopolis is so dusty and the water is so bad? Had not the umbrella better go above, and the rugs on the other seat?

Last of all, with a certain tenderness that he knows will appeal to me, where will the most gracious effendi permit him to place the dear old trap, my companion over so many thousand miles of travel? At my feet? No; on the cushion beside me!

The guard blows his whistle; the carriage doors are locked. Yapouly — Dreco Yapouly, the reformed — leans outside. I move to the window for a parting word. After all, I may have misjudged him. He starts forward, and presses some cards into my hand.

"For your friends, effendi, when they want good dragoman."

I turn up their white faces.

UNDER THE MINARETS

They are clean and newly printed, and bear
this inscription : —

ISAAC ISAACS,

Dragoman and Interpreter,

Constantinople.

A PERSONALLY CONDUCTED ARREST
IN CONSTANTINOPLE

I

CASIMIR, lifting his hat from his glistening head, said, with a bow of apology, that I could not paint — in Constantinople, of course ; that " one udder Engleesh wait one, two, four week, and t'en go 'way wit'out permit. One Russian have his machine take' away. No, effendi," he added ; " I ver' sorry, but it eempossible to make t'e picture."

" How about an American ?" I asked.

" Ah ! you not Engleesh ? You American ? T'at is anudder t'ing. I make pardon," with another sweep of his hat. " I t'ink you Engleesh." Then, behind his hand, in a whisper, " Engleesh all time make trouble."

The lowered voice and furtive glance for possible Britishers in disguise revealed like a flashlight all the devious ways and manifold crookednesses of the tourist-dragoman of the East, — your servant to-day, serving you servilely and

A PERSONALLY CONDUCTED ARREST

vilely; somebody else's to-morrow, still servile
and vile.

The clerk of the hotel agreed with Casimir as
to my painting — in the streets. So did the
banker who cashed my first draft.

The banker, however, was more lucid. In
the present condition of the Armenian question,
he said, an order had been issued from the palace forbidding any one to reproduce a likeness
of anything living or dead, from a camel to a
mosque. Special terms of imprisonment were
provided for those bold enough to outline such
persons as carried guns. Five years was the
penalty for sketching a fort; and the bowstring
or a double-shotted bag and the Bosporus for
transferring to paper the image of a man-of-war
or a torpedo-boat.

I had heard threats like these before, not
only here, but in other parts of the world. I had
been warned in Cuba, watched night and day in
Bulgaria, and locked up in Spain; and yet,
somehow, I had always kept successfully at
work, buoyed by the hope that a quiet manner,
a firm persistence, and inherent invincible honesty would carry me through.

I accordingly opened my white umbrella and
paint-box the following morning in front of the
Sultana Validè Mosque.

213

Casimir protested with hands aloft and with streaming face, a red silk handkerchief damming the flow near the chin-line. He begged me to go at once to the chief of police with him for a permit, insisting that if I were caught we should both be put under lock and key, and disporting himself generally after the manner of his guild, — one moment with vehemence, the next with dove-like gentleness. Moreover, under all his boasts and predictions I detected a genuine fear of the guardians of the peace, and a fixed determination, so far as he himself was concerned, to keep out of their clutches. This, together with his desire at all hazards to earn my five francs a day, made Casimir a very nervous and for the time being a very uncomfortable personage.

I selected for my first sketch the open plaza fronting the Sultana Validè, because it was a blossoming field of giant umbrellas, green, brown, and white, beneath which were sold stuffs and fruits of every hue in the rainbow, and because I thought that my own modest and diminutive sunshade might be so lost in the general scheme as to be undistinguishable.

The population of that part of Stamboul thought otherwise.

Before I had half blocked in one corner of

the mosque and indicated my high lights and shadows, a surging throng of Turks, Greeks, Jews, Gentiles, and Hottentots — unquestionably Hottentots, for some were as black as coal — had wedged themselves in a solid mass about my easel.

Casimir shrugged his shoulders, throwing his eyes skyward, his mouth open like that of a choking chicken. He had consented, under protest, to carry my sketching outfit across the Galata Bridge, handling it as tenderly as if it had been a bomb ; and now that it was about to explode he wished it distinctly understood by the bystanders that the affair was none of his doing. I endured this for a while, catching now and then his whispered word dropped in the ear of an eager looker-on, and then called out, —

"Here, Casimir ! Don't stand there paralyzed. Clear the crowd in front, so that I can see the steps of the mosque, and then go over to the fountain opposite and fill this water-bottle."

He obeyed mechanically. There was an opening of the crowd for a moment as he passed, a tight closing up again, and the curious mob was thicker than ever.

When he returned he brought with him two full hands. One was his own, holding the

bottle; the other was that of a gendarme holding Casimir.

The crowd in front melted away, and the
pair stood before me.

He was a small gendarme, topped with a fez,
girded with a belt, armed with a sword, and
incrusted with buttons. He wore also a sinister
smile, like that of a terrier with his teeth in a rat.
I concentrated in my face all the honesty of my
race, reached out my hand for the water-bottle,
and waved the officer aside. He really was in
the way.

The gesture had its effect; a shade of doubt
passed across his countenance. Could I be some
foreign potentate in disguise? Casimir caught
the look, and poured out instantly a history of
my life at home and abroad, my distinguished
position as court painter to the universe, my
enormous wealth, my unlimited influence, etc.
The master-stroke of dragoman policy of course
would have been to pacify the officer and satisfy
me.

There was a hurried conference, and the two
disappeared. This time Casimir held the officer
by the arm, in a wheedling, confiding way.

The crowd crystallized again, closer now than
ever. I began on the umbrellas, and had dotted
in a few of the figures, with dabs of vermilion

216

for the omnipresent fez, when an Arab who was craning his head over my canvas was unceremoniously brushed aside, and three preservers of the peace stood before me — the red-fezzed rat-catcher and two others. Casimir's face was permeated with an expression of supreme contentment. I saw at a glance that, whatever had happened, his own innocence had been established. I saw, too, that he had cut away from under my feet every plank in my moral platform. An honest expression of face, dense ignorance of the customs of the country, and righteous indignation would no longer do.

The speaker wore fewer buttons than the terrier, and had a pleasanter smile. " Effendi," he said, " your dragoman informs me that you have already applied to the Minister of Police for a permit, and that it will be ready to-morrow." This in Turkish, Casimir interpreting. "I am sorry to interrupt your work to-day, but my duty requires it. Bring your permit to my station in the morning, and I will give my men orders to protect you while you paint, and to keep the people from disturbing you."

It was beautiful to see Casimir as he translated this fairy-tale, and to watch how with one side of his face he tried to express his deep interest in my behalf, and with the other his

217

entire approval of the course the chief had taken.

The decision of the officer finished operations for the day in Stamboul and its vicinity, and cut off further discussion. The situation compelled absolute silence. Casimir's lie about his application for a permit and the chief's courtesy left me no other course. I bowed respectfully, thanked the officer for his offer, as kind as it was unexpected, lighted a cigarette, crossed the street, and ordered a cup of coffee. Casimir struck my colors — my white umbrella — and got my baggage-train in motion. I went out with my side-arms — my brushes and my private papers and my unfinished sketch — intact. The rout was complete.

"It was t'e only way, effendi," said Casimir, laying my umbrella at my feet. "But for Casimir it was great trouble for you. T'e chief was furious. We go to-morrow. I ask for permit. T'e dragoman of t'e minister is my long-time friend. He do anyt'ing for me. The permit come in one minute. Not to-day; it is too late." His recent diplomatic success had evidently emboldened him.

"But there is still half a day left, Casimir. What time does the boat leave the Galata Bridge for Scutari?"

"Every hour. Does t'e effendi wish to see t'e howling dervish ? "

"No; the effendi wishes to see the fountain at the mosque nearest the landing."

"To wash himse'f ? " — with a puzzled look.

"No; to paint."

"But t'e police ? What will Casimir do ? "

"What you *ought* to do is to get me a permit at once. What you *will* do will be to concoct another yarn. Pick up that easel; I am not going to waste the afternoon, police or no police. Quick, now ! "

So we went to Scutari. There certainly could be no crime in painting so beautiful a thing as the fountain of Scutari. If these fairy-like creations of the East were objects of worship I could easily turn Mohammedan.

This time Casimir laid aside the skin of the 'possum and wriggled into the scales of the serpent. Opposite the fountain was a low awning shading a dozen or more little square stools, occupied by as many natives drinking coffee and smoking chibouks. On one of these stools Casimir, gliding noiselessly, placed my paint-box. The umbrella was not needed, as the awning hid the sun.

This master-stroke, costing the price of a cup

of coffee, — half a piastre, or two cents, — deceived the crowd outside, as well as the police ; and the sketch was finished in peace, while Casimir drank his coffee and grew black in the face from exhausting his lungs on a chibouk. (Casimir is a Greek, not a Turk, and cigarettes, not chibouks, are his weakness.)

But my relief was not of long standing. In upper Stamboul, the next day, I was politely but firmly commanded to " move on ; " and only the intervention of a grave and dignified old priest — a vision in soft, flowing silk robes, turquoise-blue, pale green, and lemon-yellow — prevented my being marched off to the nearest station for investigation.

I felt that the situation was beyond any former experience. I must either present myself at the office of the Minister of Police and plead for a permit, or close my outfit and give up work.

II

At the end of a flight of wooden steps crowded with soldiers, a long, wide hall, and a dingy room, I found the chief dragoman of the Minister of Police — not a dragoman after the order of Casimir, but a dragoman who spoke seven languages and had the manners of a diplomat.

In Constantinople there are of course dragomans and dragomans. Each embassy has one
as an interpreter. Many of them are of high
rank, the German dragoman being a count.
These men, as translators, are intrusted, of
course, with secrets of great moment. Every
consulate has a dragoman, who translates the
jargon of the East — Arabic, Turkish, modern
Greek, Bulgarian *patois*, and the like — into
intelligent English, French, or German ; and so
has every high native official with much or little
to do with the various nationalities that make
up the Ottoman empire and its neighbors.
There are, too, the modern guides called dragomans, who interpret in many tongues, and who
lie in all.

When appealed to, this high-caste dragoman
of the minister said evasively that he believed
he remembered Casimir — he was not sure. It
was necessary, however, for me, before approaching his Excellency, to be armed with a
passport and a letter from my consul vouching
for my standing and integrity. Something might
then be done, although the prospect was not
cheering ; still, with a wave of his hand and a
profound bow, he would do his utmost.

I instantly produced my passport, — I always wore it in my inside pocket, over my

heart, — and at once called his attention to the cabalistic signature of the Turkish official who had viséd it on the day of my arrival — three wiggles and a dot, a sign manual bearing a strong resemblance to an inch-worm scaling a tree.

The next day — there is not the slightest hurry in the East — I handed in my second document, emblazoned on the seal with the arms of my country, and certifying to my peaceful and non-revolutionary character, my blameless life, and the harmless nature of my calling.

The minister was in; I was asked to take a seat outside.

The outside was the same hall, bare of everything but officers, soldiers, and hangers-on. At one end stood two men with worn-out stubs of feather dusters, who pounced upon every pair of shoes that entered the sacred precinct, giving each two quick polishing strokes — one piaster for Casimir's and mine. At the other end hung a great red curtain, covering the door of the minister's office, patched and bound with leather, as stiff as a theatre-drop, and guarded by an officer in full uniform. My passport open, my character indorsed, my shoes dusted and the dusting paid for, I was ready for his august presence. The curtain was drawn aside, and I stepped in.

Seated at a common folding-desk littered with papers, surrounded by secretaries and officers, sat a man perhaps fifty years of age, with calm, resolute, clear-cut face, and an eye that could have drawn the secrets from a sphinx. He was neatly dressed in dark clothes, with plain black necktie. The only spots of color about him were a speck of red in his buttonhole and the vermilion fez that crowned his well-modelled head. In his hand he held the consul's letter and my passport and visiting-card. For an instant he bored me full of holes, and then with a satisfied glance motioned me to a seat. Casimir, who had preceded me, was bent double in profound obeisance, his head almost on the floor. I returned his Excellency's glance as fearlessly as I could, and sat down to look him over. At this instant a clerk entered with some papers and advanced rapidly toward his desk. The interruption evidently was inopportune, for the same eye that had comprehended my entirety shot an angry look at the intruder, who stopped, wavered, and then, shrivelling up like a scorched leaf, glided back out of the room. Not a word was spoken by either. The power of the eye had been enough. It was only a flash glance

223

that I got, but it revealed to me one of the hidden springs of this man's dominating will. Here, then, was the throttle-valve of the Ottoman empire. When the Sultan moved the lever this man set the wheels in motion.

He listened patiently, scanned the papers keenly as I talked on, the sinuous, genuflecting Casimir putting it into proper shape, and then handed me a cigarette. I lighted it, and rambled on, explaining how, four years before, when my sketching outfit and baggage had been overhauled by two officers at the station, doubtless by his Excellency's orders (he bowed slightly, but gave no other sign as to the truth of my surmise), I had personally called the attention of these officers to a sketch made above the navy-yard, with all the men-of-war and torpedo-boats left out, as I considered that I had no right to transfer them to my canvas; and how both had then been satisfied, and left me with apologies for the examination. He raised his head at this, and covered me with one sweep of his eye, from my dusted shoes to my bared head. Then he played with his cigarette for a moment and said slowly and thoughtfully, —

" Come to-morrow at one o'clock."

I spent the remainder of that day sketching about the old walls of Seraglio Point, making

224

snap-shots with my sketch-book, dodging the police along the water-front of Stamboul, idling about the cafés, and in and out of the narrow streets packed so full of people that I could with difficulty push myself through. I could easily believe the statement that there are more people to the square foot in Stamboul than anywhere else on the globe.

At noon the following day I again had my shoes dusted, and again cooled their heels for an hour outside the swinging mat. One o'clock was *my* hour, not that of his Excellency.

When I was at last admitted the minister came forward and extended his hand. Casimir braced up and got his head high enough to see over the desk.

"I cannot grant your consul's request to give you a permit," he said in a calm voice. "In the present disturbed condition of affairs it would establish a precedent which would afterward cause us trouble."

Casimir's face, when he translated this, looked as if it had been squeezed in a door. The threatened collapse of all his rosy plans seemed to take the stiffness out of his neck.

"I have decided, therefore, to detail an officer who will personally conduct you wherever you wish to go. I shall rely upon your good

225

judgment to paint only such things as your experience teaches you are proper.''

Casimir's back now humped up like a camel's,
and his face beamed as he interpreted. He did
not, of course, put the minister's speech in these
words — he mangled it with a dialect of his own ;
but I knew what the soft, musical cadence of
the minister's voice meant. Then his Excellency
went on, —

" The officer selected is one of my personal
staff. He will be at your hotel in the morning
to receive your orders. *Au revoir*.''

When I crossed the Galata Bridge the following morning I was attended by two men, — one
the ever-suppliant Casimir, carrying my outfit
as triumphantly as if it contained the freedom
of the city, and the other a thickset, broad-
shouldered man, with a firm, determined face
and quick, restless eyes, whom the gendarmes
saluted with marked respect as we passed.
This was Mahmoud, attached to the minister's
personal staff, and now detailed for special duty
in my service. He was responsible for my conduct, the character of my work, and my life,
with full power to strike down any one who
molested me, and with equal power to hurry
me to the nearest lock-up if I departed a hair

line from the subjects which, by the graciousness of his chief, I was permitted to paint. The
sketches I made would never have been possible except for his ceaseless care and constant
watchfulness of me. A Mohammedan crowd is
not always considerate of an infidel dog, especially when he is painting sacred mosques and
tombs. Moreover, stones are convenient mis-
siles when such giaours are about.

III

But there were days when Mahmoud was not
with me, days at Therapia, a little nestling
village strung around a curve in the shore line
of the Bosporus, with abrupt green hills rising
about it, — with beautiful gardens, delightful
groves, and flower-bordered walks, its banks
lapped by water of marvellous clearness and
purity, fresh with every tide from the Black
Sea.

This Newport of the East was founded some
centuries ago by the Greeks because of its in-
vigorating climate, — Therapia signifying health,
— and to-day is still the refuge in the summer
heats not only of many of the pashas and other
high Turkish dignitaries whose palaces line the
water-front or crown the hills near by, but of
scores of European wayfarers and strangers who

want more air and less dog than can be found in Pera.

Here, too, are the houses of the several foreign embassies, — English, German, French, and the others, — their yachts and dispatch-boats lying at anchor almost in front of their gardens, the brasses glistening in the sun.

And the charm of it all! The boats' crews of Jack Tars in their white suits rowing back and forth, answering calls from the shore ; the blue water — as blue as indigo — dotted with caïques skimming about ; the dog-carts and landaus crowding the shore road, with footmen in gorgeous Albanian costumes of white and gold, and with sash and scimitar, — all make a scene of surprising brilliancy and beauty. Diplomacy is never so picturesque as at Therapia.

There is, too, a superb hotel, — the Summer Palace, aptly called, — with shaded rooms, big overarching pines, tennis-courts, ball-rooms, and bath-houses, besides all the delights of yacht and caïque life.

This Summer Palace, with its spacious drawing-rooms and broad terraces, is thronged nightly not only with members of the diplomatic corps, with their secretaries and attachés, — daily in touch with questions of vital importance, yet never unmindful of the seductions of gliding

228

slippers and waving fans, — but also with officers of the imperial army and navy, members
of the Sultan's cabinet, and other high officials
immediately connected with his Majesty's government. The perfect repose of manner and the
easy, unassumed dignity of these Turks, especially of the younger men, are to be expected,
for Orientals are never hurried or nervous; but
their graciousness and gentleness, and, more
than all, their unconscious simplicity, — a simplicity that comes only to men trained to good
manners from their infancy, just as they are
trained to swim, to ride, and to shoot, — were,
I confess, revelations to me.

At these gatherings in the Summer Palace
there were, of course, no Turkish women; but
there were plenty of others — Greeks, Armenians, and Europeans — crowding the rooms
all day and filling the cotillions at night. If his
Majesty passed sleepless nights at the palace
ten miles away, worrying over the latest de-
mands of the Powers, there was no sign of it
at Therapia. The merry hours went on. The
caïques were nightly filled with bevies of young
and old, singing in the moonlight. There were
tennis matches, afternoon teas, excursions by
land and water, and all that goes to the
making of the life of pretty women and gallant

men having no stronger ties than those born of mutual enjoyment, and apparently weighted with no duties more arduous than the killing of time.

And there were other days without Mahmoud at Stenia, a few miles from Therapia, to which place I once took ship — the daintiest little ship, all cushions and rugs, manned by two boatmen in white balloon trousers, with yards and yards of stuff to each leg, and Greek jackets embroidered with gold. And from Stenia to the "Sweet Waters of Asia," an Arabian Nights sort of place, with an exquisite Moorish fountain of marble, and great trees shading flocks and bunches of houris in white yashmaks and embroidered feredjès of mauve, yellow, and pink, out for an airing from their harems ; all on mats and rugs spread on the grass, attended by black eunuchs, with hands as black as terrapins' paws, and as wrinkled and leathery.

The almond - eyed beauties chattered and laughed and munched bonbons and partook of rose-leaf jelly, sitting with their tiny feet tucked under them, Turkish fashion, their cigarettes perfuming the still air, until their caïques gathered them in again, and they all floated away like so many colored swans. You must not wander too near. Even a faithful Turk turns his head away when he passes a woman : a Christian dog might miss his just above the collar button for forgetting the courtesy.

Neither was Mahmoud with me when I went to the Greek Fair, within a mile of the Sweet Waters, and that beautiful fountain, around which sit the more beautiful houris, whose eyes shine large and luminous through thin veils.

This day the air was delicious, the sky like a delft plate, with puffs of white clouds in high relief. For hours I watched the merry-go-rounds, and the jugglers on their mats, until I grew hungry enough for even a Greek café, — and it is a brave and reckless appetite that dares an Oriental kitchen.

This café was under a tree, with a few pine boards for a table, the galley being within handing distance, with a charcoal fire blazing. The abominations of stew and fry and toastings were intolerable ; but I succeeded in getting a box of sardines and half a pint of native wine, a loaf of bread and some raw tomatoes and salt, with a bit of onion, which I gathered up and spread out on the pine boards. When the combination of chef, head waiter, and proprietor, all covered by one fez, presented his bill, it amounted to a sum that would have supported an Oriental and his family for a month.

A PERSONALLY CONDUCTED ARREST

There are occasions when your individual pantomime is more effective than the closest translation of your spoken words. Mine to mine host ended in an abrupt turning on my heel, with hands tightly clenched. When the crowd began to take sides with the Greek and matters assumed an ugly look, I threw upon the ground a silver coin equal to one fourth of the charge. This turned the tide, — the bystanders considered the sum too appallingly large even for a Greek fair !

Here, too, I had my fortune told by a Tzigane from the desert, — a real gypsy in baggy trousers of calico and little bare feet, with silver bangles around her ankles, and with a blue silk handkerchief wound loosely about her head. She had rings of turquoise in her ears and rings of silver on her fingers, and, for aught I know, tinkling bells on her stubby, dust-covered toes. She held my hand in a caressing way, and passed her own over it softly, and looked at me with her large, deep eyes, and told of the fair-haired man and the letter that would come, and the dark-eyed woman who loved me, picking out from a bag, as she talked, now a nut, now a pebble or a bit of broken glass, and spreading them on her lap. Her incantation began with only one piastre as a talisman, —

mine, of course, — but it required two francs in addition before the fair man of whom she had warned me was outwitted and the dark eyes were made happy. Casimir interpreted all this with an expression of contempt and disgust on his face wholly out of proportion to the occasion, and entirely unjust, I thought, to the dust-soiled priestess who thus read my future. But then the francs did not go Casimir's way.

Although Mahmoud did not follow me to Therapia, where I spent the nights, he was waiting every morning for me in Stamboul at the Galata Bridge, the gangplank that unloads Europe into Asia, and *vice versa*, every hour of the day and night. When I landed in this district I was his prisoner. One day he led me to the Plaza of the Hippodrome, — the Atmeidan, — with its twin needles of stone; another day to the west façade of the Mosque of Sultan Ahmed; again to the Court of the Pigeon Mosque, and to the Mosque Bajazet, the Mosque of Suleiman the Magnificent, and the others.

Casimir, of course, was always within hand touch of Mahmoud when the morning boat from Therapia was made fast. It was his craning head which appeared first over the red sea of fezzes climbing the wide landing-plank, — one hand on my luggage, the other shading his eyes.

Next I would perceive Mahmoud, grave, dignified, attentive. Then we would all three make
our way through the throng, take a tram in
Stamboul, and slowly mount the hill to St.
Sophia. Before the week was out the police had
come to know the posse of three. The priests,
too, who at first were dubious about the honesty of my intentions, and who demurred at the
sacrilege of my painting their mosques, now saluted me in passing. The people of the streets,
though, were still as curious as ever, crowding
about my easel with eyes staring in wonder.
But if they pressed too close, a word in an un-
dertone from Mahmoud melted the crowd away
or awed it into respectful silence.

When the muezzin called from the minaret,
and the faithful laid down their work and
moved into the mosque to pray, Mahmoud went
too. After the first day he discarded his uniform, all but his fez, for a suit of light gray, exchanging his short sword for a stout stick. This
stick Casimir held as his badge of office while
Mahmoud prayed.

I followed him once into the Mosque of
Ahmed, and watched him as he knelt, barefoot,
his face to the stone wall, his lips moving in
prayer, his eyes on Mecca, his forehead touching the mats. This bloodthirsty savage! This

234

barbaric Turk whom we would teach morals and
manners ! I can imagine how hoarse a muezzin's
throat would become calling the Broadway
squad to prayers, if his duty compelled him to
continue calling until our police should fall upon
their knees in the nearest church.

Now and then Mahmoud would buy a loaf of
bread and feed the dogs — not his dogs, not
anybody's dogs, only the dogs of the streets.
It is a mistake to call these dogs scavengers;
but for the kindness of the people they would
starve. If some highly civilized Caucasian
should lose his temper when one of these hungry, homeless curs looks up into his face, and
use his boot or his cane in reply, it would be
Mahmoud's duty promptly to convey the highly
civilized person to the nearest station, from
which the chief would instantly send him to
jail for a year. When a child stumbles and falls
in the street the nearest man springs forward
to save it. When a father enters a son's presence, though he be as ragged as Lazarus and as
dirty as a scavenger, the son remains standing
until he has permission to be seated. And yet
in my own land we build ten-story buildings
side by side — one to prevent cruelty to animals,
another to children, and a third to provide
against the neglect of the aged !

235

A PERSONALLY CONDUCTED ARREST

Mahmoud's watchfulness of me was not over until I packed my luggage for Venice and he was called upon to give an account of his stewardship to his chief, the Minister of Police.

I can see him now, standing that last day in the doorway of the station, waving his hand. His final courtesy was to return me my passport *unopened* by the guard at the station. The air with which he placed this much-be-inked document in my hands conveyed to me even more clearly than his translated words how fully he had appreciated my docility while a prisoner in his hands, how sorry he was to have me leave, and how entirely unnecessary and useless such vouchers were between men who knew each other so well. Strange to say, the chief inspector at the frontier thought so too, returning it with a bow and a look instantly intelligible to me, — knowing Mahmoud as I did.

And besides that of Mahmoud there was one other face, or rather part of a face, — his back was toward me, — of which I caught sight as I whirled out of the station.

It was Casimir's.

He was biting one of the coins I had just given him to see if it was good.

THE HUNGARIAN MILLENNIUM

I

"IF monsieur will walk upstairs, the most private rooms are on the second floor ; " this with a wave of a napkin hung over his wrist and folded like a bath-towel.

I followed up a richly carpeted staircase, soft and velvety to the tread, past mirrors concealing muffled doors, down a long hall hung with pictures and lighted by softened electric lights, through an archway draped with silk curtains, and into a cosey room filled with small tables resplendent in white linen, spotless silver, and polished glass. He drew out a chair, placed the *menu* before me, and took that lop-sided, deaf-in-one-ear attitude generally assumed by a tall waiter listening breathlessly for your opening order.

In the interval between soup and fish I began to look about me. The walls were panelled with mirrors ; the ceilings were covered with pink cupids diving into banks of white clouds.

There were chandeliers of crystal, sideboards of ebony, and bunches of chrysanthemums ; there were candlesticks of silver, with candles topped by red silk shades ; there were relays of finger-bowls and whole arsenals of forks and spoons ready for instant service, besides all the other appurtenances, appointments, and equipments of a restaurant, so exclusive and costly that one would have supposed that none but a plutocrat or a stranger from out of town dare enter it.

Opening from this inner room was a smaller apartment — I really had to pass through it to reach my own seat — where a table was spread for ten or a dozen expected guests. Here were more shaded candles and a great basket of roses, while at every other plate was laid a bunch of violets tied with a purple ribbon.

As my roast and one vegetable were laid before me — it was a table d'hôte at a fixed price, wine extra — an important-looking personage entered the smaller apartment and glanced critically at the waiting table. He was an elderly man, with a white mustache waxed into needle-points, a very red face, and bald head. From his chin to his waist-band and as far east and west as his armpits, an unbroken snow of waistcoat, shirt, tie, and collar stretched in one trackless sheet of white. In the centre of the drift was a single diamond glistening like an icicle.

A moment afterward a stout lady entered, evidently the wife of the important personage, — a stout lady in yellow satin, with black feathers and pearls, who dropped little cards at the several plates, and disappeared through the curtained archway and into the velvety corridor. All this time the personage was examining the labels on a battery of bottles masked behind a sideboard.

With my pease — table d'hôte pease are always a separate dish in this part of the world — came the rustle of silk and the bubble of talk, broken by little gurgles of laughter as the expected guests appeared. The important personage led the way, with a woman on his arm as beautiful as any to be found in all Europe, and followed by a procession of handsome and well-dressed people, the rear being brought up by the stout lady in yellow satin, escorted by one of those square-shouldered, tight-laced, pipe-stem-legged young officers so often seen in Vienna, in the Volksgarten, or along the Ringstrasse.

With the serving of my coffee and cheese, the merriment of my neighbors was at its height.

Every one was laughing, talking, reaching under the clusters of roses to touch one another's
glasses, keeping up a rattling fire of good-
natured badinage, all in an unknown tongue,
while each and every one seemed as unconscious of my presence — I sat within ten feet
of the personage's chair — as if I had been a
painted cupid myself suspended in mid-air above
their heads.

With the bringing in by the waiter of the
paper containing the sum of my indebtedness,
and my payment of the fixed price, — I laugh
now when I think how small it was, — I arose
from my seat and passed the merry table on
my way out, with that abashed, noiseless, no-
business-to-be-there tread common to all men
in a like situation. To my astonishment, the
personage also rose, saluting me graciously, his
guests at the same time pausing in their talk,
each face reflecting the courtesy of the host,
while I, doubled up with badly executed bows,
passed into the velvet corridor, with its pictures
and rose-colored electric bulbs, and so downstairs, and out upon a wide boulevard lined by
palaces, thronged by gayly dressed people, and
brilliant with myriads of lights.

Out where? On one of the great boule-
vards of Paris — the Capucines, or perhaps

the Champs Elysées itself — or possibly upon the sidewalk of Unter den Linden in Berlin, or the Ringstrasse of Vienna?

Guess again, my friend. This boulevard has twice as many people at this hour of the night as the Champs Elysées; is altogether more beautiful than the Ringstrasse, and infinitely gayer than the Unter den Linden. Besides all that, underneath its surface runs the most perfect electric railway in the world, with stations every few blocks, reached by flights of steps descending from the sidewalk, stations lined with pure white tiles and lighted by electric lights, while at the far end stretches a park, in which is placed the most satisfying and instructive exhibition of recent times, the Exposition of the Millennium of Hungary.

For it is in neither Paris, Berlin, nor Vienna that I have dined so delightfully and been so overcome with the courtesies of strangers. On the contrary, it is in that little split-in-two town on the Danube, seven hours by rail east of Vienna, the city of Buda-Pesth, its old Oriental half clinging to the heights of Buda on the one bank, and its more modern half, the city of Pesth, spread out over the other.

You are surprised, doubtless, at the surroundings I have described, — the café, the guests, the wide, gayly thronged street. You had an idea that Hungary was one of the out-of-the-way places of the earth, inhabited by strolling gypsy bands playing on queer instruments; that it was browsed over by herds of goats and sheep attended by barelegged shepherd boys blowing Pan-pipes. You fancied, perhaps, that its only productions were certain brands of mineral waters of highly pronounced and widely advertised medicinal properties, or odd varieties of silver bangles and girdles worn by male and female peasants shod in high boots, into which are tucked trousers of unusual width and looseness.

If you have thought none of these things, I frankly confess that I have.

Before I had been in Buda-Pesth many hours, however, I felt my preconceived notions vanish. With a bewilderment that never left me while I was in Hungary, I walked out upon the wide boulevard, the Andrássy-üt, and looked back at the Café Drechsler, where I had just dined, a really superb building of light stone incrusted with carvings and decorated by life-sized statues. Further progress up the Andrássy-üt increased my wondering admiration. In almost every block I found other spacious cafés, ablaze with lights and thronged with other gayly dressed people, not in impossible baggy trousers and boots, but in French bonnets and Worth dresses, all sipping their coffee as they listened to the weird strains of Tzigany music, with its hesitating notes, intricate crescendoes, and nervous soarings, — a music so infectious and inspiring that hardly a slipper was still. Every now and then I came upon an octagon, which widened the broad thoroughfare into a "place" with a Hungarian name all z's and c's, surrounded by great apartment houses and hotels, their broken roof-lines massed against the sky in picturesque effects altogether different from those produced by the endless mansards of Paris in their never-varying height. Still further up the street were the lights of spacious city villas, with gardens and big trees, while at the very end — a sweep of a half-circle, its diameter line marked by a series of towers hung with banners and festooned with myriads of colored lanterns — was the main gate of the Exposition.

Night is not the best time to judge of an exhibition of this kind, I said to myself as I neared the entrance. Night is too forgiving; its masses of shadows conceal too tenderly. Night is never really honest. Even its artificial high lights add to the sins of its kindly deception.

The glimpses that I caught were, to be sure, all inviting. There were vistas of winding gravelled walks, ablaze with electric lights, and stencilled here and there with the black shadows of overbending trees outlined against the sky; avenues of great marble palaces fretted over with Oriental tracery, and ending in broad flights of steps guarded by big bronze figures; clusters of magnificent domes, minarets, and towers.

But my better judgment and my former experiences taught me to weigh these effects before giving free rein to my enthusiasm. I knew something of the power of the gas-man and of the scenic painter. The same tricks I had seen played elsewhere were being used here, except that this background was the deep blue of the starlit night, instead of the canvas drop of the stage. Many an architectural sham, all of painted boards or deceptive plaster, could be concealed, I knew, by a well-hung lantern or the shadow of a well-draped flag, while minor details could be none the less cleverly managed. Only a year before, in Vienna, one night, I had seen my own beloved Venice so charmingly reproduced, with its canals, gondolas, old palaces, and quaint streets, that I was fool enough to believe the very pigeons on the window-sills were sound asleep, until I examined them the next

day in broad daylight, and found them but
lumps of painted clay.

Yet, for all my better judgment, I walked on
here at Buda-Pesth, looking about me in wonder, gazing up at the myriads of lifeless flags
hanging limp in the soft night air, until I found
myself opposite the little ticket-kiosk, beyond
which no human soul could pass without paying
an admission fee — none except beatified direct-
ors, royal families, and holders of official passes.

"How many tickets shall I take out of this
twenty-mark gold piece?" asked the young
lady, in very good French.

"One this time, if you please;" and I
passed in, with nineteen marks left in my
pocket.

But even though I thought myself deceived
by the illusions of the night, I found it impossible to resist the fascination of further discovery.

One building puzzled me, even in the glam-
our of the twinkling lights — or, rather, one
group of buildings. They were built on the
margin of the lake, and were reached by a
sanded plank and painted portcullis. The first
story was genuine — at least so I thought; for
I am mechanic enough to know good masonry
when I see it, even in the dark, and the turning of the groined arches, all in honest red brick

245

stained by age, savored more of the trowel than of the brush. But the top courses, I was sure, were of canvas and cheap boards. (This building had its full revenge on me the next day, when I caught the morning light glinting on its shingles of *real* slate.)

I had caught, too, something of the contagious humor of the crowd as it wandered and loitered. I lingered with it for a moment by the grand music-stand, where sixty musicians were blowing and pounding away to their hearts' content and the listeners' delight; I mingled, too, with it as it passed the Hall of Liberal Arts — an immense building, its broad flights of steps thronged with people — and walked with it around a huge fountain, with its water-jets ablaze with color, and followed it when it pressed a passage into another building, in which one of the innumerable foreign congresses was having a banquet.

I had seen some of the members of this congress a few hours before at the Hotel Hungaria, in the city proper: white-bearded fellows, most of them, with bumps all over their foreheads, deep-set eyes, and hair cut, or uncut, à la Wagner; some wearing glasses, and hardly one without a speck of red or green or blue in his buttonhole — old fossils these who had spent their

246

lives in catching glimpses of stars that had been dodging for ages behind planets or careering through space. And younger ones, too, with inflamed eyes and gaunt faces, who had choked half the vitality out of their bodies by noxious smells and compounds.

They were all here inside this building when I came upon them, but they were not peering through telescopes nor bending over retorts. On the contrary, they were listening to some high dignitary of Buda-Pesth, who was telling them how proud and happy it made the Buda-Pesthers (that's my coinage) to welcome them to the heart of Hungary. He had told the same thing, it is true, in slightly different phrases, every week for months, to dozens of other congresses, representing every known science and craft, from biology to market-gardening; but to-night, as if the welcome were entirely new, every member of the present body rose and cried, "Hear! hear!" (each one in his own tongue), and drank bumpers of champagne, and sat down again to listen, now to a Herr Professor from Dresden, now to some Don from Madrid, replying in French — that language suiting best the largest number of delegates — expressing an undying sense, etc., etc., and the never-to-be-forgottens, etc., etc., common to

247

such occasions. And the crowd with which I had forced a way into the galleries cheered too, in its gay, impulsive way, while I caught the humor again and waved my own handkerchief as I clung to a pillar and looked on.

Nobody below waved back to me in return, moved up as if to make room, filled a flagon, nor did anything else in my honor; and so, feeling myself for the second time that night but an observer of happy people's pleasure, I wedged my way down again and out into the fairy-like scene, and stopped at an open-air café — Gerbeaud's Royal Pavilion — a café more gorgeous than any I had seen; all garden, with palms and flowering plants, dotted here and there with small tables sheltered by enormous lace parasols, under which one could sit and sip ices and coffee, besides no end of queer concoctions known only to the Magyars. The pavilion itself, with its fine portico and spacious wings, its dining-rooms, great and small, and its verandas enclosed by glass, filled one end of the garden. The waiter told me in whispers that the Emperor comes here, and the Archduke and Duchess, and pointed out the very chairs in which his Majesty sits. When the bill for one ice and one glass of plain water was presented, I realized how good it must be to reign, a

THE HUNGARIAN MILLENNIUM

potentate with unlimited power to levy taxes;
for no ordinary exchequer could stand the strain
were a man really hungry.

All that had saved me from utter bankruptcy
— this being a café in the exhibition, not in the
city — had been my natural antipathy to eating
anything dropped alive and kicking over burning coals. For the head waiter, to tempt me as
I came in, had passed in front of me with a live
thing flopping on a plate, — it was a fish this
time, just out of the water, — and had stopped
just long enough to allow me a rapid glance at
its beauty. I at first supposed that some lucky
line had but a moment before drawn it struggling from the lake, and that it was being taken
to die elsewhere. It was only when I overheard
the minute instructions for its immediate and
proper serving — it was handed to an epicure at
the next table to mine — that I was undeceived,
and it was not long before I discovered that
such fish formed one of the chief attractions of
the place. I then began to watch, from where
I sat, the small boy who, in the centre of the
café, presided over the fountain under the blazing gas-jets, dipping his net into the marble-lined
pool, chasing the dodging fish round and round,
until some unlucky victim of the right size
slipped into the mesh, and was flopped wriggling

on a plate. The sight had rather dulled my appetite. It was as if some one had driven in a spring lamb and had asked me to carve out a brace of chops while the little fellow waited. I had the curiosity, however, to inquire the price of this gastronomical luxury. It equalled that of two bottles of Extra Dry — the price being the same to commoners and to kings !

The night sped on, the fascination of studying a new life still holding me. The lake was alive with boats, the bands were never out of one another's hearing, and the crowds were surging everywhere.

When the big bell sounded for closing, the people instantly obeyed, and the stream of sightseers turned and began to flow back to the gate.

Then came the rush for the underground electric railway, one of its stations being almost opposite the main entrance of the exposition. These stations are small houses, fifteen by twenty feet square, and resting on the sidewalk. Once inside, you descend a flight of stone steps leading to an underground room, lined, as I have said before, with white tiles, the frieze and dado of majolica in rich colors. There are comfortable seats against the wall

for waiting passengers, and double gates, of
spirally turned iron with brass ornaments, protecting the farther end. Across the double-
tracked road is another tiled room protected by
similar gates. These two sets of double gates
make a kind of pound, in which thirty-two
passengers are corralled, as it were, or a less
number if some of the car seats are occupied.
When a train stops, the middle door of the car
slides back, and the contents of the pound walk
leisurely aboard. There is no crowding and no
jostling. There are no bent elbows aimed at
your waistband, no hanging to straps, no making half a parenthesis of your body that a stout
woman with a basket may pass while you still
keep tight hold of your overhead brace. Every
passenger has a wide and comfortable seat,
cushioned with velvet. The cars themselves
are of mahogany or hard-wood ; the lights are
brilliant ; the road-bed as smooth as a floor.
Each car starts as gently as a yacht with loosened sails, and slows down without a tremor.
The movement known as the "Third Avenue
Cable Jerk," with the passengers shot into one
end of the car like the contents of a steamer
trunk on a rough night at sea, is unknown. The
ventilation is perfect, for there is no smoke, and
consequently no smell. In fine, it is the poetry

of motion on wheels, smooth as a gondola, and almost as noiseless.

My train stopped within a few blocks of the "Hungaria" — there are underground stations all up and down the Andrássy-üt. The white-bearded scientists with bumps on their fore-heads, and the younger ones with inflamed eyes, had already arrived, and were gathered together in jovial groups in the hotel's spacious corridor. They had evidently dined well, for some were without any very definite or helpful vertebræ, and others had apparently lost the use of the knee-joint. Many of the younger ones, while they lacked a certain directness of vision, had gained immeasurably in volume of voice, and were, at the moment of my arrival, engaged in rehearsing their several national airs. Scattered about were the generous Buda-Pesthers, — every man as straight as a ramrod.

The hospitality of the Magyars is proverbial. So are their staying powers. The only things ever under their tables are the empty bottles, and now and then a guest.

II

The purpose of the founders of this National Millennium Exhibition is best expressed, per-haps, in the words of Minister Lukács, Minister

252

of Commerce (do not for one moment suppose the translation is mine !) : —

"The government (he says) will take care that the national work be exhibited in a worthy frame, so as to further the interest of the exhibitors. May every one of you, its subjects, therefore show what he is able to attain by his diligence, his taste, and his inventive faculty. Let us all, in fact, compete — we who are working, some with our brains, others with our hands, and others with our machines — like one man for the fatherland.

"This will be a rare family festival, the equal of which has not been granted to many nations. Let the people gather, then, round our august ruler, who has guided our country with fatherly care and wisdom in the benevolent ways of peace to the heights which mark the progress of to-day, and who — a faithful keeper of the glorious past of a thousand years — has led the Hungarian people to the threshold of a still more splendid thousand years to come!"

There was no question about the response of the people. Simultaneously with the opening ceremonies, thanksgiving services were held in the different churches throughout the empire. Gala performances were afterward given at the theatres and opera-houses, the programmes of

which included dramas, plays, and operas, written for the occasion by Hungarian dramatists
and composers, while regattas, races, and sports
of all kinds came in quick succession. In addition to these merrymakings a series of congresses assembled, with representatives from
all parts of the world, many coming from the
United States. These special congresses succeeded one another in rapid succession, and were
attended by journalists, historians, actors, tour-
ists, athletes, as well as philanthropists, scientists, and engineers.

The interest evinced in the exhibition itself,
as well as in each of its many features, extended
all over the empire. Not only from Buda-Pesth,
but from all the country districts the peasants,
as well as the nobility and gentry, gathered to
enjoy it. In its provision for these peasants, the
direction, backed by the government, showed
great liberality and forethought. It maintained
that as this exhibition was for the education of
the people, poverty must not prevent their enjoyment of the privilege. Special accommoda-
tions were accordingly provided for the peasants; railroad fares were reduced or abolished
altogether, and arrangements were made by
which a peasant living within a hundred miles of
Buda-Pesth could visit the exhibition, be fed,

lodged, and conducted through the grounds and buildings by competent guides, for the space of two days and nights, at an expense of five florins all told, or about two dollars of our money. Moreover, pupils of schools and teachers were given free passes, with all living expenses paid, it being considered important that no educator in Hungary should miss the exhibition for want of means to see it. These privileges existed during the entire life of the exhibition, which lasted for six months, and which was visited by nearly four millions of people.

It is seldom one sees such patriotism allied to such progress; for although Hungary is celebrating its one-thousandth anniversary, Buda-Pesth itself was not born until 1872. Ancient Buda, on the right bank of the Danube, remembers many centuries, it is true, and the modest little town named Pesth, on the left bank, has also seen many years. But the united, splendid, modern city of Buda-Pesth, with its present population of over six hundred thousand inhabitants, is really but twenty-five years old.

Neither can there be any question of the way in which the lovers of Buda-Pesth regard their city. Listen to Alexander Bródy, a distinguished Hungarian author (again some one else translates — please remember this): —

"I liken Buda-Pesth to a beautiful woman, fascinating and spirituelle, and it is to the beautiful women of Buda-Pesth that I pay homage. The capital abounds with them, of all sorts and conditions. At times it seems to me that some one must have collected and selected all the various types of beauty of the world and congregated them here in our city streets and suburban walks. . . . I have occasionally gone in search of their less favored sisters, the ugly ones ; but they are conspicuous by their absence, and so too are the thin and the pale. . . .

"We Hungarians are a new people. We are moral, young, interesting, and peculiar. We have much to show in the way of sights, and we are rich in things the study of which would amply repay the trouble bestowed. Our actors are geniuses ; our press is versatile ; our public statues are lamentably bad ; every second house is a restaurant or café, which we are incessantly abusing ; and yet, as far as eating and drinking are concerned, there is no place to equal Buda-Pesth in the excellence and cheapness of its *cuisine*. Such is the sober and industrious Hungarian metropolis, immersed in popular song and drowned in the clash of its gypsy music."

I admire the distinguished author's enthusiasm, but I cannot agree with his statement that

there are no "thin and pale" countenances to
be seen among these women. I must in all sincerity draw another picture. I caught its outlines, not in one of the crowded cafés or along
the Boulevard or down by the side of the blue
Danube, but up a back street in one of the new
quarters of the rapidly growing city. I had seen
the same sight in Bucharest the day before, and
knew what it meant. Brick and mortar, and the
many ways of lifting them up and down, have
always interested me. I know the slow, measured tread of big, red-shirted Pat, as he clum-
sily climbs the vertical ladder, the hod on his
shoulder, and can still hear from the bricklayers
above the cry of " Mort " sifting down between
the unfloored beams of the several stories. I
know, too, the more modern hoist, where a turn
of the lever sends both brick and mortar flying
skyward to the scaffolding overhead. But a girl
of sixteen and a grayhaired woman of sixty
were new types of brick and mortar carriers to
me. And not in one place alone, but wherever
a building is in course of construction.

Narrow platforms instead of ladders are made
for them, running zigzag up the outside scaffolding. The mortar (all mixed by women)
is dumped into a tub, a pole is thrust through
the handles, swung over the shoulders of two

257

women, and the weary climbing to the top be-
gins. I saw one dark-eyed, barefooted girl, —
she was pale and thin enough, — clothed only
in a skirt and chemise, rest the tub for a moment at the first landing and press her hand to
her side as if in great pain, the older one waiting for her patiently.

With all its beauty, dash, and enthusiasm,
it must be a curious civilization which tolerates
and makes possible a sight like this. It made
my blood run cold and hot. It was as if one had
ploughed with a fawn.

But this custom, hideous as it is, cannot, I
think, be counted for many more years against
these people. Their progress in social order is
too marked, let us hope, to permit of a long con-
tinuance of this degradation.

III

I have seen nearly all the great exhibitions
of the last twenty years, but never in any of
them such order and such cleanliness as prevailed in this. I was prepared, after my hurried
night inspection, to be a little critical, my enthusiasm of the night before having led me so far
the other way. But there was nothing tawdry
to be seen : nothing that the impartial light of
the next day revealed to me as a disappointment,

VARIED TYPES OF HUNGARIAN ARCHITECTURE.

or to which the night and its shadows had lent a charm the sunshine stole.

Broad and shaded walks, perfectly swept and watered, separated the several pavilions and structures. Only in the historical group did one see any massing of buildings. This group included three wonderful palaces, connected together, and illustrating varied types of Hungarian architecture — the pointed arch, the Renaissance, and the rococo. It was reached by a bridge on stone piers, thrown across an arm of the lake, and connecting with the portcullis of the nearest building. It had all the appearance of having stood there for centuries, and of being able to stand for as many more. Not only had a genuine antique finish been added, but all those telltale chippings of mortar and "staff," showing the grinning laths, had been here carefully avoided, which at the close of our own World's Fair revealed only too clearly the ephemeral nature of the construction of almost every building. From bed-stone to weather-vane this historical group had the air of hoary age, quite as if lichens grew in the cracks, and lizards darted in and out of the fissures. It is the work of the Hungarian architect Ignacz Alpár, the genius of the exhibition.

Externally it presented not the slightest evidence of its hasty construction, nor did it suggest a temporary use. The parts intended as permanent could not be distinguished from the painted shams, so skilfully had the architect done his work.

No haste was apparent in the workmanship of the other buildings; every structure of importance looked as if it had taken years to build, and had only been improved by careful delay.

As I idled on through shady walks, two other pavilions came into view : the Hall of Industry filled with exhibits of furniture, ceramics, and glass, besides manufactures of leather, woven fabrics, jewelry, domestic and decorative arts, and the pavilion of Bosnia and Herzegovina, a perfectly proportioned building, rich in color, and of exquisite Oriental design, containing the manufactures of those provinces.

And the other exhibits were no less interesting than the structures which housed them. They were of course wholly Hungarian, no foreign products or manufactures having been admitted. Even the special capacities of their enormous rolling-mills could easily be judged by a glance at an enormous steel rail, measuring in length, I should think, some seventy-five feet, and rolled at one heat ; a huge steam-plough, and a monster locomotive designed for climbing steep

mountain grades. There were, also, every variety of equipage, tons of beet sugar, coal, ore,
and soap, miles of cloth, yarn, and silk, hogs-
heads of wine, and bushels of every grain that
could grow on a stalk; but the seventy-five
foot steel rail in one piece told a story of the
capacity and accompaniments of furnace, rolls,
and hammers that set at rest all preconceived
notions of the primitiveness of these people.

I came, too, upon the customary fountain,
common to all exhibitions of this class. Here it
was treated in a novel and somewhat interesting way.

It was erected in the open space fronting the
Hall of Industry. From an enormous basin of
water rose a huge pile of rough rocks heaped
together in pieces varying in size from that of
a piano to that of a chair. Life-size figures of
nymphs, mermaids, water-sprites, and sea-gods,
cast in imitation of bronze, clambered in and out
among the rocks. Over these grotesque and
sometimes picturesque figures great jets of water were constantly thrown. At night, when the
spray was tinted with many-colored electric
lights, these figures looked like elves and sprites
peering out of the red glare of a Christmas pantomime.

The Museum of Fine Arts — no exhibition

is complete without one — stood outside the main entrance. We on our side of the water know of course the work of Munkácsy and his pupils, but it would surprise and delight our students and connoisseurs to wander through these spacious galleries and see how many other interesting painters are to be found in Hungary. Their names, unfortunately, are almost all unpronounceable, and to me unspellable, but their paint-signatures are as plain as print to any one who can recognize a new touch and the beginning of a new school as distinct and individual as the Russian or Swedish. One of these painters — Arpád Feszty — had painted a panorama representing the first invasion of the earlier tribes, and produced a sky so luminous and apparently so many miles in depth that it is impossible for the observer who stands on the circular platform and looks out, to realize that a live swallow sailing into the deep azure would necessarily dash his brains out against the painted canvas in a flight of less than twenty feet.

Altogether the Millennial Exhibition of the Hungarians carried a lesson well worth the studying. As a record of a people whose whole history has been one long struggle for independence, and who have so recently attained, if not complete autonomy, certainly the right to manage their internal affairs in their own way, without paying too high for the privilege, it showed unparalleled native skill united to marvellous intelligence.

Everything had been done in a thoroughly substantial way, without any straining after cheap and bizarre effects. Whatever had been attempted, whether in the reproduction of some famous cloister loved by the nation, or the doorway of a well-known castle revered in their traditions, had been made as genuine as the restrictions of expense would permit, the object having been to create a reproduction which would afford pleasure and profit to peasant and savant alike.

The strongest impression produced upon me was that of the earnest, honest effort shown by the government and its agents to make the exposition helpful to the people themselves, not only as an educational factor, but as proving to them how important in all that pertains to the liberal arts is their position among nations, and how marvellous has been their progress since their real freedom began.

The two strong notes I felt were the paternal and the patriotic.

IV

Of course there was still another department
— there always is at every well-regulated exhibition, whether centennial or millennial. This
was the department of the nondescript, the un-
classified, and the heterogeneous. With us it
was known as the Midway Plaisance ; at Buda-
Pesth it had the suggestive name of Ös-Budavár.

Here was a department of astounding wooden
houses, cardboard mosques, and unlimited cafés
— the kind where the pine tables are constantly
wet with beer, and the same mugs do for all
day with but a single dip in water. The entrance was through a gate — a conglomerate
mass of turrets, portcullis, bastions, massive
canvas masonry, and painted bricks. Once inside and the hurdy-gurdy began.

There were imitation Turks, with fez and
baggy trousers ; there were imitation Venetian
gondoliers, male and female this time, with
Neapolitan caps and Tyrolean skirts ; there
were Turkish smoking-rooms, with rugs and
nargiles on sale at moderate prices, attended
by houris speaking pure Hungarian ; there was
a mosque in imitation of nothing on earth in
which a Mussulman ever said his prayers — a

bare interior with a wainscoting of stencilled tiles and walls of canvas, with make-believe Orientals squatting on mats. There were side-shows concealed by a carpet curtain, outside of which stood a Nubian or a New Zealander or a Hindoo, just as the management determined, one and the same swarthy Magyar doing ser-vice for all during the season ; he brandished a scimitar one day and beat a tomtom the next, while every and all day he cried aloud the vir-tues and attractions of the performance within. There was Madame Aultightz, the marvellous Polish beauty, whose sole costume was a suit of stockinet without a wrinkle, buttoning under her chin, around her wrists, and below her ankles, and who did Venuses and nymphs, but drew the line at draped Victories and Milos. There was also Herr Dubblejawnts, the Aus-trian contortionist, who twisted his legs and arms around his neck until the whole looked like a tinted diagram in a medical book. And there were, besides, dozens of other marvellous and wonderful sights, especially appealing to the wide-eyed, open - mouthed peasants, who wandered about hand in hand in groups of ten or twelve, in their rough, homespun, home-made clothes, escorted by an officer of the army in faultless uniform and white gloves, who

265

explained to each one the several objects of interest with as much patience and kindness as if the court itself had been under his personal protection.

Cheap shams and tawdry buildings were everywhere, until I came to one place which seemed dirty and sloppy enough to be genuine. This was the Congo village with its villagers. The settlement had been made in an enclosure by itself, fenced off from the non-paying outside world by a high Robinson Crusoe stockade. Once inside, and the delusion was as complete as if one had landed from Stanley's launch with the laudable object of exchanging beads and whiskey for elephants' tusks.

The village had been built in a grove covering an acre or more, and was enriched by a great mud-puddle in the middle. About its shores and against the Robinson Crusoe stockade was a collection of huts, exactly like those we used to see in old geographies. Outside their doorways squatted the natives. There was no question about their race or their nationality ; there was no possible chance for concealment — they wore too few clothes, the children wearing none. They were veritable Congo negroes — big lips, nose-rings, and all.

When I entered, a dozen or more were seated

266

in a row on rude benches. They were singing a low chant, keeping time to the beats of half a dozen tomtoms made of gourds and tight-stretched skins. In front was a young negro, naked except for a breech-clout — a fellow beautifully formed, colored like a brierwood pipe, and straight as an arrow. He held in his hand a few green leaves, something like leaves of corn. These he waved over his head, his feet moving in unison with the weird music, his body swaying gracefully. He was singing a song, of which my dear friend Glave would, I know, have understood every word. Beside him walked a stalwart negro, much older, and of heavier build. About this man's body was wrapped a square of calico as large as a bedspread; this he kept winding and unwinding, wearing it now like a toga, or now trailing it in the dust.

All over the grounds were the other natives, peacefully pursuing their several avocations. One young mother had just girded her square of calico about her waist, and, with her little black baby — black as India-rubber — glued to her shiny back, had seized a rude axe (the same one sees in a museum), and bending over, had begun chopping the wood for the evening fire. The little tot, without other support, stuck to its mother's skin, holding on to the crinkling flesh, twisting its head to right and left to keep its equilibrium, while the mother apparently took as little notice of its efforts as if it had been a securely strapped papoose.

While her arms swung the axe, I could see that her feet kept time to the music of the tom-tom. As she caught my eye she smiled, and chopped away the harder, but she could not avoid an occasional double-shuffle.

When I put a small coin into the baby's fist, she threw down the axe and ran towards her husband, who was crouched over a heap of coals, the baby bouncing up and down like a loosened knapsack on a flying soldier. The man raised himself erect, and with one finger gouged the coin from the child's hand as if he had been opening an oyster, bit it, and bent over in thankful obeisance until his forehead touched the ground. Then he regained his seat among the embers, the smoke curling up between his knees. When I drew closer I found that he had just finished anointing his mahogany legs with some kind of hot oil, and was now hard at work putting on a piano finish with the palms of his hands.

Here at last was the savage untouched by civilization, unspoiled by the isms and fallacies of nineteenth - century progress ! Here were simplicity and primeval human nature ! In the midst of the shams of Ös-Budavár the entire genuineness of the whole place was refreshing.

My attendant joined me at this moment — my guide, in fact — and shook hands with the Congo man. Then, noticing the African shivering with cold, this conversation took place, in plain, unvarnished English, —

"Pretty cold, John, is n't it ? " said my guide.

"Cold ! — I dinkey so — damn cold ! " replied the Congo man.

"You speak English ? " I asked, in astonishment, of the Congo man.

"Yes, me speakee."

"Who taught you ? "

"De good missionary at home, he teachee me."

I had been mistaken, the stamp of civilization was on him too !

On my way back to the Underground Electric Railway that afternoon I fell in with another congress. One could hardly help falling in with some of them, they were so scattered. The dinner this time had been in the middle of the day, and they were once more in search of the

Hungaria. Their Magyar hosts were doing the piloting, — straight as gendarmes and as sober.

Far into the night, from my room under the roof, I could hear the voices of these congress-men singing their national songs.

The Magyars alone were silent: they were on duty.

Their singing days would begin when the fair was over.

A BULGARIAN OPERA BOUFFE

HE was a small waiter with a slightly bald head, and of no very pronounced nationality, and he spoke the fag-ends of five or six languages, one of which, I was delighted to find, was my own.

These fragments he hurled continuously at other waiters of more pronounced nationalities — French, German, Hungarian, and the like — who were serving little groups of Turks, Russians, and Bulgarians scattered about the coffee-room.

Directly opposite me hung a half-length portrait of a broad-shouldered young soldier bristling with decorations, his firmly set features surmounted by a military cap.

"Is that a portrait of the prince?" I asked.

The man of many tongues stopped, looked at the chromo for an instant, as though trying to remember to which one of the late princes I had referred, and then said blandly, —

"Yes, monsieur; the present king, Prince Ferdinand."

271

"Is he now in Sofia ?"

The slightly bald attendant elevated his eyebrows with a look of profound astonishment.

"Here ? No, monsieur."

"He has really run away, then ?"

The eyebrows fell, and a short, pudgy finger was laid warningly against his lips.

"Monsieur, nobody runs in Bulgaria. His majesty is believed to be in the monastery at Ryllo."

"Yes, so they tell me. But will he ever come back here ? "

The man stopped, gazed about him furtively, refilled my glass, bending so low that his lips almost touched my ear, and then whispered, with a half laugh, —

"God knows."

I was not surprised. All Europe at that precise moment was straining its ears to catch a more definite answer. The conundrum was still going the rounds of the diplomats, and the successful guesser was yet to be heard from.

All that was positively known concerning his imperial highness was that several weeks prior to the time of this writing he had left his palace at Sofia, the capital of Bulgaria, — within musket-shot of where I sat, — and, attended by a few personal friends, had taken the midnight express to Vienna. From Vienna he had gone to Carlsbad, where for several consecutive weeks he had subjected his royal person to as many indoor baths and as much outdoor exercise as would entirely eradicate the traces of gout and other princely evils absorbed by his kingship during his few years' stay in the capital of the Bulgarians.

All this time the air had been full of the rumor of his abdication. The Russian ambassador at the court of Paris, Baron Mohrenheim, in an interview granted to the Paris correspondent of a St. Petersburg paper, insisted that there was no doubt that Ferdinand had quitted Bulgaria for good, " his life there being in constant danger." While the Austrian ambassador at Constantinople, Herr von Radowitz, was reported to have advised the Porte to postpone taking action on the Bulgarian Note for the present, hinting at the imminent retirement of the reigning prince, and a consequent solution of impending difficulties more in harmony with the purport of the Berlin Treaty.

These announcements continued, and with such persistency that the Bulgarian prime minister, M. Stamboloff, deemed it necessary to telegraph to a newspaper correspondent, " The rumors of the prince's intended abdication are pure fabrications."

More emphatic still was Ferdinand's own manifesto, issued through the columns of the Carlsbad "Temps," to the effect that " while there is a great national effervescence going on at this moment in Bulgaria, the Bulgarians are, nevertheless, free, and will welcome me back with rejoicings."

It was while this political "effervescence," as the prince was pleased to call it, was at boiling point that the royal liver grew torpid enough to demand a change of air. This torpidity lasted, in fact, long after the Carlsbad doctors had pronounced the diseased organ cured. You will remember that Talleyrand tried the same experiment with similar results nearly a century before.

Then one day the prince turned up serenely on the slopes of the mountains, dismounted like a weary knight, and knocked for admission at the monastery at Ryllo.

Being myself a wanderer in this part of the world, with an eye for the unexpected and picturesque, and anxious to learn the exact situation in Bulgaria, I had hurried on from Buda-Pesth, and at high noon on a broiling August day had arrived at a way station located in the midst of a vast sandy plain. This station the conductor informed me was Sofia. Following my trap through a narrow door guarded by a couple of soldiers, I delivered up my ticket and passport, crept under a heap of dust propped up on wheels and drawn by three horses abreast with chair-backs over their hames, waited until a Turk, two greasy Roumanians, — overcoated in sheepskins wrong side out, — and a red-necktied priest had squeezed in beside me ; and then started off at a full gallop to a town two miles away. Our sudden exodus obliterated the station in a cloud of dust, through which the Constantinople express could be seen slowly feeling its way.

The interview with the waiter occurred within an hour of my arrival.

The same afternoon I was abroad in the streets of Sofia armed with such information as I had gathered from my obsequious attendant.

In the king's absence I would call upon the members of the cabinet.

It did not take me many hours to discover that his Excellency M. Stamboloff, Minister President, was away on a visit, presumably at Philippopolis ; that the Minister of Justice, M. Salabashoff, had resigned a short time before ;

275

that Doctor Stransky, Minister of Foreign Affairs, had followed suit, the portfolios of both being still unassigned ; that the Minister of Finance was in Varna, the Minister of War, Colonel Moutkourov, in Vienna. In fact, that not a single member of the Bulgarian government, from the king down, was to be found at the capital. The Bulgarian government had apparently absconded. Not a member, not a representative, was to be found, unless a gimlet-eyed man of about forty, with a forbidding countenance, a flat military cap, and a tight-fitting white surtout encrusted with gilt buttons, who answered as prefect of police, might be so considered.

I ran up against this gentleman before I quitted the palace grounds. He had already run up against me at the station on my arrival, — as I afterward discovered, — and had entered me as a suspicious character at sight.

In five minutes he had bored me so full of questions that I became as transparent as my passport, which he held up to the light in order to read its water-mark. Next he went through my sketch-book page by page, and finally through all my letters until he came to one bearing at its top the image of the American eagle and at its bottom the superscription of one of its secretaries, answering for my sobriety, honesty, and industry ; whereupon he waved me to the door with full permission to roam and sketch at my will. Then he put a special detective on my track, who never took his eyes from me during any one of my waking hours.

I did not ask this potentate whether the prince was coming back. I did not consider it an opportune moment.

Neither did I discuss with him the present condition of Bulgaria, there being nothing in the cut of his coat — nor of his eye, for that matter — to indicate his present political views. He might have been an adherent of the prince, or a believer in Panitza, or a minion of Stamboloff, or he might have been so evenly balanced on the edge of events as to be all three or none.

Nor did I explain to him how grieved I was that his present lords and masters should have seen fit to absent themselves just at the precise moment when their combined presence would have been so agreeable to me. I had really crossed desert wastes to study their complicated comedy, and now all the principal actors were out of town.

A rehearsal of the preceding acts of this play may possibly lead to a better understanding of the drama as it was then being developed in

Bulgaria. It is not heroic; it cannot even be called romantic, this spectacle in which three millions of souls are seen hunting about Europe for a sovereign, — a sort of still hunt resulting in the capture of two kings in four years, with hopes of bagging a protector or a president before the fifth is out.

But to the play itself.

At present in Bulgaria there are, first, the Russophiles, who, as Petko Karaveloff says, "pray for the time when Bulgaria shall march into Salonica, while Russia marches into Constantinople," and who believe the Czar to be their natural friend and ally, with the only hope of settled peace in his protectorate. Secondly, the loyal oppositionists, headed by M. Radoslavoff, who would support the prince with certain concessions, but who detest his advisers. And thirdly, the sympathizers of Major Panitza, the murdered patriot, who was "shot" — so ran a proclamation a week old, patches of which were still pointed out to me decorating the walls of the king's palace — "by the order of the bloodthirsty Ferdinand, the scoundrel Stamboloff, and the 'Vaurien' Moutkourov."

This young officer, Panitza, — a devoted adherent of Prince Alexander, — had served with distinction in the Servian war, having led one of the famous charges at Slivnitza. Believing that the only salvation for his country lay in Russian interference, he had joined hands with a Russian spy, Kolobkoff, in fomenting discord in the army. Unluckily, his own letters, carrying unmistakable evidence of the plot, fell into the hands of Stamboloff himself, resulting in his immediate arrest, trial, and condemnation by court-martial.

It is greatly to the credit of Prince Ferdinand that he was strongly inclined to spare Panitza. He in fact held out for more than a week against the combined assaults of Stamboloff and his brother-in-law, Moutkourov, — then minister of war, — and it was not until his prime minister threatened the resignation of the entire cabinet that he finally yielded. There is even a story current that when this threat failed, Stamboloff followed the king to Lom Palanka with the death-warrant in his hand, and that when he still hesitated that implacable dictator remarked sententiously, —

"Sire, Major Panitza dies on the morrow. If you continue to object, there is one thing we can always do for your majesty, — we can always buy you a first-class ticket to Vienna."

Stamboloff's plan for governing had been simple and to the point. It called for five millions of roubles and a king. Who this king might be, or where he should hail from, was a matter of detail. Anybody but a Russian or a Turk would do. And so offers were made in a confidential way to various gentlemen who thought they had an especial, divine gift for reigning, and who lacked the opportunity only because of the depleted condition of their bank accounts. At last a fond and ambitious mother and an obliging son with an almost unlimited reserve fund — unlimited for the ordinary needs of life — took the bait.

It was not, however, a harmonious family arrangement; for it was well known that the young prince's uncle, the Duke of Saxe-Coburg, did what he could to prevent the final agreement, — he being an older and wiser diplomat, and having had a long and varied experience in the ups and downs of several see-saw governments. Among other things, the duke boldly stated that it was only a question of money with the Bulgarian regents, and that Ferdinand would leave the throne when his guldens were gone, as had Alexander, to whom the Bulgarian government then owed three millions of francs.

The duke was right. When the hour arrived,

there were, of course, cogent reasons for heavy drafts on the king's exchequer, — the army was to be rearmed and clothed, an important railroad built, and a thousand and one improvements made. The money would be returned.

This schedule has been literally carried out, — except the return item, — if not to the benefit of Bulgaria herself, certainly to the depletion of the prince's bank account.

Among the most seductive of these schemes was the beautifying of the capital. Streets were to be opened, and trees planted, and flowers made to bloom. I recall now that vast band of stagnant dust leading from the station to the town, separated from its surrounding monotony by sundry depressions and grades indicated along the line by the excavated débris which fringed its edges; with a double row of infant trees marking its curb-lines, each one of which was shrivelled to a crisp by the blistering heat. Added to this mockery, at regular intervals stood flower-beds in ovals, and diamonds, and circles, filled with plants burned to a cinder, — their very blossoms, which no man had dared pluck, dead for months, and still standing brown and dust-begrimed.

Such is the great boulevard leading from the railway to the palace !

The boulevard, however, is not the only part of Sofia illustrating the prevailing taste to overturn and reconstruct. One sees it in the new part of the town, where government buildings, bare, white, and forbidding, are going up in all directions. One sees it also in the old mosque and garden landmarks left standing high above new streets now being cut to their very edges; their preservation a tacit acknowledgment of their right to exist, their isolation a forerunner of their death, — quite as the old traditions are being undermined by the present government.

Many of these streets serve a double purpose. They make a short route to the palace, and they provide right of way for hasty artillery practice. One cannot always tell, in so changeable a climate as that of Bulgaria, when the prevailing political wind may shift.

The palace itself, a great hospital-looking building surrounded by a garden, suggests only stately discomfort and emptiness. In walking through its great halls and scantily furnished salons, I could not help pondering upon the peculiarities of human nature, and wondering what could have induced this fine young officer — and he is a fine fellow in every sense of the word — to give up his brilliant life in Vienna, the most delightful capital in Europe, and to a young man of fortune the most fascinating, in order to bury himself in this ugly pile of masonry. But then the market is never overstocked with empty thrones, while would-be kings are a drug.

The old part of the town, however, is still quaint and Oriental, and has thus far escaped the restless shovel and saw. It lies in the dip of a saucer-shaped valley, surrounded by bare brown hills. Netted with crooked, dirty streets and choked with low, shambling houses, with here and there a ruined mosque, it remains a picturesque reminder of the days of Turkish rule, unchanged since the signing of the Berlin Treaty, when in a single year five thousand of Mohammed's chosen shook the dust of Sofia from their feet and sought refuge under the Sultan.

The most interesting of these quaint remnants of Oriental architecture found in the old part of the city is the Mosque Bania-bashie, dating back to the year 1279. This mosque is still the resort of the devout Mohammedan, who prays therein five times a day with his face towards Mecca, and who, despite the restrictions that vex his race, still prostrates himself on the floor of the mosque below, in obedience to the call of the muezzin from the slender minaret above.

Here I had my first glimpse of Mohammedan

worship, and to one unaccustomed to the forms of the Mohammedan religion, and especially to one who sees them for the first time, I know of no religious spectacle more impressive. Before you stands a barefooted Turk erect on his prayer-rug, with his face toward Mecca and his eyes looking straight into the eyes of his God. You see at a glance that it is not a duty with him, nor a formality, nor the maintenance of a time-honored custom. It is his very life. Watch him as he enters this wretched interior of Bania-bashie, with its scaling and crumbling walls, and its broken windows, through which the doves fly in and out. Outside, at the trickling foun-tain, he has washed his feet and face and hands, bathing his throat and smoothing his beard with his wet fingers. He is a rough, broad-shouldered, poorly clad man in fez and skirt, his waist girt with a wide sash, ragged and torn. He is per-haps a "hamal," a man who carries great weights on his back, — a human beast of bur-den. His load, whatever it may be, is outside in the court. His hourly task is his daily bread ; but he has heard the shrill cry from the mina-ret up against the sky, and stops instantly to obey.

He enters the sacred building with his shoes in his hands. These he leaves at the edge of the mat. Now he is on holy ground. Advancing slowly, he halts halfway across the floor, and stands erect. Before him is a blank wall; beyond it the tomb of the Prophet. For a moment he is perfectly still, his eyes closed, his lips motionless. It is as if he stood in the antechamber of Heaven, awaiting recognition. Then his face lights up. He has been seen! The next instant he is on his knees, and, stretching out his hands, prostrates himself, his forehead pressed to the floor. This solitary service continues for an hour. The man stands erect one moment, with a movement as if he said, "Command me; I am here;" the next he is prostrate in obedience. Then he backs slowly out, and, noiseless, regains his shoes, bends his back to his burden, and keeps on his way, his face having lost all its tired, hunted look.

There is no mistaking the impression made upon you. It is not a religious ceremony, nor a form of devotion, nor a prayer. This man has been in the very presence of his God.

Next to this crumbling mosque stands the Turkish bath, with its round dome pierced with bull's-eyes, through which the light falls in slanting parallel bars upon clouds of boiling steam. The water gushes from the ground at a temperature of 110° Fahrenheit, the pool being shoulder-deep and filling the whole interior excepting the narrow edge, around which cling the half-boiled natives in every variety of undress uniform from the pattern used in the Garden of Eden down to the modern dressing-gown.

Outside of this circular room are cooling apartments smelling of wet towels and furnished with divans upon which men lounge, half-clad, smoking cigarettes. Now and then from an inside cubbyhole come the whiff of a narghile and that unmistakable aroma, the steam of smoking coffee.

What a luxury after a four months' drought and its consequent accumulation of Bulgarian dust! How genuine and unique this volcanic-heated symposium compared to all its base imitations palmed off on a suffering public in the several capitals of Europe and America! For more than six hundred years, and in fact before the mosque was built, has this pool of Siloam comforted the sick and soothed the well and cleansed the soiled. And hot, too, — boiling hot out of the ground, running free night and day, and always ready, with its accompaniments of Turkish coffee, pipes, and divans. Go to, with your marble slabs, and radiators, and high-pressure boilers under the sidewalk!

Beyond this section of narrow streets there

runs a broad highway lined with booths attended by all sorts of people — Gypsies, Turks, Jews, Greeks, and Hungarians, selling every kind of merchandise entirely worthless to anybody but a native. Here are rings of bread, squares of leather for sandals, messes in bowls with indescribable things floating about in boiling grease, heaps and lumps of other things served smoking hot in wooden plates, and festoons of candied fruit strung on straws and sugared with dust. Here are piles of melons and baskets on baskets of grapes, — these last delicious, it being the season, — and great strings of onions, pyramids of tomatoes, and the like. Everywhere is a mob in rags, apparently intent upon cutting one another's throats to save half a piastre.

Farther on is the Jews' quarter, the street Nischkolitza, with its low houses eked out by awnings under which sit groups of people lounging and talking, and behind these, in little square boxes of rooms let into the wall, squat the money-changers, — their bank accounts exposed in a small box with a glass top, through which can be seen specimens of half the coinage and printage of eastern Europe.

If the king's continued absence caused any uneasiness among the people crowding these streets and bazaars, there was nothing on the surface to indicate it. Many of them looked as if they had very little to lose, and those who had a little more either carried it on their persons in long chains of coins welded together, — a favorite form of safe-deposit with the Bulgarians, — or, like the money-changers, hived it in a portable box.

Nor could I discover that any one realized that he was living over a powder magazine with a match factory next door. On the contrary, everybody was good-natured and happy, chaffing one another across the booths of the bazaars, and bursting into roars of laughter when my brush brought out the features of some well-known street vender.

The only native who really seemed to possess any positive ideas on the uncertain condition of public affairs was a Polish Jew, the keeper of the bath, whom I found berating two soldiers for refusing to pay extra for their narghiles, and who expressed to me his contempt for the ruling powers by sweeping in the air a circle which embraced the palace and the offenders, spitting on the floor, and grinding his heel in the moistened spot.

Near the bath, and in fact almost connected with it by a rambling row of houses, is one of the few Oriental cafés left in Sofia, —a one-story building with curious sloping roof, its one door opening upon the street corner. It is called the "Maritza." On both sides of this entrance are long, low windows shaped like those of an old English inn, and beneath these — outside on the sidewalk — is a row of benches, upon which lounge idlers sipping coffee and smoking cigarettes. Within are a motley crew of all nationalities, liberally sprinkled with Bulgarian soldiers out on a day's leave.

Coffee is almost the only beverage in these Turkish cafés. It is always handed you scalding hot in little saucerless cups holding hardly a mouthful each. A glass of cold water invariably accompanies each cup. This coffee is generally the finest old Mocha, with an aroma and flavor unapproachable in any brand that I know, except perhaps the Uruapam coffee of Mexico. In preparing it the roasted bean is ground as fine as flour in a hand-mill, — a teaspoonful of the powder, with half the amount of fine sugar, being put into a brass pot with a long handle. To this is added a tablespoonful of boiling water. The pot is then thrust into the coals of a charcoal fire until the coffee reaches boiling point, when it is caught up by the waiter, who runs to your table and pours the whole into your cup.

Although it is dark and thick, it is never strong, and there is not a wakeful hour in a dozen cups.

To me there is nothing so interesting as one of these Oriental cafés, and so I turned in from the street, drew a square straw-covered stool up to a low table, and held up one finger. A fez-covered attendant shuffled over and filled my cup. As I raised it to my lips, my eyes caught the riveted glance of a black-bearded man with a beak-like nose and two ferret eyes watching me intently. He was dressed in a half-cloak orna-mented with a dark braid in twists and circles, and wore a slouch hat.

Being stared at in a café for the first five minutes is so usual an experience for me, in my tramps abroad, that I accept it as part of the conditions of travel. But there are, of course, different kinds of stares, all induced and kept up for the most part by idle curiosity, which gen-erally ceases after my dress has been examined, and especially my shoes, and when my voice has been found to be like that of other men.

This man's stare, however, was devoid of curiosity. His was the face of a ferret; a sly, creeping, half-shrinking face, with an eye that pierced you one moment and slunk away the next. The thought flashed through my mind — a Spanish Jew who hides his gold in a hole, and who is here changing money while the "effervescence" lasts. When I looked again, a moment later, he had disappeared.

The face haunted me so much that I traced its outlines in my sketch-book, trying to remember where I had seen it. I finally persuaded myself that it only suggested some similar face seen long ago. Finishing my coffee, I lighted a cigarette, picked up a stool, and, planting it across the street, began a sketch of the exterior of the café.

The usual crowd gathered, many following me from the room itself, and soon the throng was so great that I could not see the lower lines of the building. No language that I speak is adapted to Bulgaria, and so, rising to my feet, I called out in honest Anglo-Saxon, —

"Get down in front!" This accompanied by a gesture like a policeman's "Move on."

Nobody got down in front, or behind, for that matter. On the contrary, everybody who was down got up, and the sketch was fast becoming hopeless, when four gendarmes arose out of the ground as noiselessly and mysteriously as if they had issued from between the cracks of the paving-stones, formed a hollow square, with the café at one end and me at the other, — the intervening space being as clear of bystanders as the back of my hand, — and stood like statues until the sketch was finished. When I closed my book half an hour later, a man on the outer edge, wrapped in a cloak, raised his hand. The crowd fell back, a gap was made, and the four gendarmes passed out and were swallowed up.

I turned and caught a glimpse of a black hat half concealing a dark, bearded face. It was my friend of the café. Not a Spanish Jew at all, I said to myself, but some prominent citizen respected by the police and anxious to be courteous to a stranger. And again I dismissed the face and the incident from my mind.

Just here another face appeared and another incident occurred, neither of which was so easily forgotten. The face enlivened the well-knit, graceful figure of a young man of thirty dressed in a gray travelling-suit and wearing a derby hat. Every line in his good-natured countenance expressed that rarest and most delightful of combinations, — humor and grit. From this face proceeded a voice which sent down my spine that peculiar tingle which one feels when, halfway across the globe, surrounded by jargon and heathen, he hears suddenly his own tongue, in his own accent, spoken by a fellow-townsman.

"I heard your 'down in front' and knew

right away where you were from ; but these Bashi-bazouks blocked the way. My name is Burton, correspondent of the ' Herald.' Been here two months watching this mouse-trap. Come into the café, where we can talk. You don't know what a godsend an American is in a hole like this."

An interchange of cards settled all formalities, and when, half an hour later, numbers of mutual friends were discovered and inquired after, we grew as confiding and comfortable as if we had been the best of friends through life.

Burton was one of those men of whom everybody hears, whom few people see, and not many people know ; one of those men whose homes are fixed by telegrams, whose wits, like their pencils, are sharpened in emergencies, whose energies are untiring and exhaustless, who ransack, permeate, get at the bottom of things, and *endure,* — individual men, sagacious, many-sided, and productive, whose whole identity is mercilessly swallowed up and lost in that unnoticed headline, "Our Correspondent."

I had heard of Burton in Paris a few weeks before, where his endless resources in the field and his Arctic coolness in tight places were by-words among his fellow-craftsmen. At the time his friends supposed him to be somewhere between Vienna and Constantinople, although none of them located him in Bulgaria, great morning journals being somewhat reticent as to the identity and whereabouts of their staff.

"Yes," he continued, "life here would reconcile a man to the bottomless pit. I was in London doing some Irish business, — rose in your buttonhole at breakfast, Hyde Park in the afternoon, and all that sort of thing, — when a telegram sent me flying to Paris. Two hours after, I was aboard the Orient express, with my shirts half dried in my bag, and an order in my inside pocket to overhaul Stamboloff and find out whether the prince had left for good, or was waiting until the blow was over before he came back. You see, the Panitza affair came near upsetting things here, and at the time it looked as if the European war circus was about to begin."

"Did you find Stamboloff?" I asked.

"Yes. Reached the frontier, learned he had left Sofia, and, after travelling all night in a cart, got him at Sistova, and caught our Sunday's edition three hours later. Here I have been ever since, waiting for something to turn up, and spending half my nights trying to get what little does turn up across the frontier and so on to Paris. And the worst of it is that for four weeks I have n't had a line from head-quarters."

"What! Leave you here in the lurch?"

"No; certainly not. They write regularly; but these devils stop everything at the post-office, open and re-seal all my private letters, and only give me what they think good for me. For two weeks past I have been sending my stuff across the frontier and mailing it in Servia. How the devil did you get permission to sketch around here?"

I produced the talismanic scroll with the water-mark and the image and the superscription, and related my experience with the prefect.

"Gave you the freedom of the city, did he? I wager you he will go through your traps like a custom-house officer when you leave, and seize everything you have. They have been doing their level best to drive me out of here ever since we published that first interview with Stamboloff, and they would if they dared. Only, being a correspondent, you see, and this being a liberal, free monarchy, it would n't sound well the next day.

"Come, finish your coffee, and I 'll show you something you can never see outside of Bulgaria."

295

We strolled up past the bazaars along the boulevard, stopping for a moment to note the cathedral, with one end perched up in the air, — Stamboloff's commissioners of highways having lowered the street grade at that point some twenty feet below the level of the porch floor.

Opposite this edifice was the skylight of the local photographer. The old, familiar smell of evaporating ether greeted us as we entered his one-story shop, — it would be a poetic license to call it a gallery, — and the usual wooden balcony, with its painted vase and paper flowers, grinned at us from its customary place behind the iron head-rest.

Here were portraits of the prince and his mother, Princess Clementine, and of poor Panitza, — whom I really could not help liking, traitor as he was to Stamboloff, — and the rest of the notables, not forgetting the dethroned prince, Alexander of Battenberg, all of whom had occupied the plush armchair, or had stood behind the Venetian railing, with the Lake of Como and Mont Blanc in the distance.

Burton hunted through the collection of portraits scattered about the table, and handed me two photographs, — one of a well-built, handsome man with pointed mustache, dressed in the native costume and shackled with heavy chains fastened to his ankles. He was standing in a prison yard, guarded by a soldier holding a carbine.

"Good-looking cutthroat, is n't he? Might be a diplomat or a night editor? Too honest, you think? Well, that's Taco Voyvoda, the famous bandit who was caught a few years ago in the act of murdering a detachment, and who was filled full of lead the next day at the government's expense. Now look at this," and he handed me the other photograph.

I held it to the light, and a shiver ran through me. On a box covered with a piece of canvas rested the head of a man severed from the body. One eye was closed. The other was lost in a ghastly hole, the mark left by a rifle-ball. The mustache was still stiff and pointed, one end drooping a little, and the mouth set firm and determined. The whole face carried an expression as if the death agony had been suddenly frozen into it. About the horror were grouped the bandit's carbine, holsters, and cartridge-belt bristling with cartridges. The belt hung over the matted hair framing the face.

Burton watched me curiously.

"Lovely souvenir, is n't it? The day after the shooting they cut off poor Taco's head, and our friend here," pointing to the photographer, "fixed him up in this fashion to meet the popular demand. The sale was enormous. Bah! let's go to dinner."

My new-found friend had a better place than the one presided over by my slightly bald waiter with the Tower of Babel education. He would take me to his home. He knew of a garden where a few tables were set, girt about with shrubs and sheltered by overhanging trees that had escaped the drought. At one end was a modest house with a few rooms to let. His gripsack was in one of these. That was why he loved to call it his home.

Soon a white cloth covered a table for two, and a very comfortable dinner was served in the twilight. With the coffee the talk drifted into the present political outlook, and I put the universal conundrum, —

"Will the prince return?"

"You can't tell," said Burton. "For myself, I believe he will. He must do so if he wants to see his money again, and he can do so in safety if Stamboloff succeeds in carrying the elections next month, which I believe he will. If he fails, the nearer they all hug the frontier the better; for there are hundreds of men right here around us who would serve every one of them as the soldiers did Taco Voyvoda. They know it, too, for they are all off electioneering except the prince, who, I understand, has left Ryllo to-day for Varna. He is hanging on the telegraph now. Not the poles, but the dispatches.

" The worst feature of the situation is that most of the factions are backed up by Russian and other agents, each in their several interests ready to lend a hand. To-day it is a game of chess between Russia and Turkey; to-morrow it may involve all Europe. Through it all my sympathies are with the prince. He has been here now nearly three years trying to make something of these barbarians, and so far not a single European power has recognized him. He will get nothing for his pains, poor fellow. When his money is all gone they will bounce him as they did Battenberg.

" Certain members of the cabinet are not safe even now," continued Burton. " While I was at Sistova, the other day, I had an opportunity of seeing some of the risks that Stamboloff himself runs, and also how carefully he is guarded. He was in a café taking his breakfast. As soon as he entered, a tall sergeant of gendarmes with his sabre half drawn and his red sash stuck full of pistols and yataghans moved to his right side, while another, equally ferocious and as heavily armed, guarded his left. Then the doors were blocked by half a dozen other gendarmes, who watched everybody's movements. There is really not so much solid fun being prime minister in Bulgaria as one would think."

While Burton was speaking three officers entered the garden where we were dining and took possession of an adjoining table. My friend nodded to one of them and kept on talking, lowering his voice a trifle and moving his chair so that his face could not be seen.

The Bulgarians were in white uniforms and carried their side-arms.

The next instant a young man entered hurriedly, looked about anxiously, and came straight towards our table. When he caught sight of me he drew back. Burton motioned him to advance, and turned his right ear for a long, whispered communication, interrupting him occasionally by such telephone exclamations as "Who told you so? When? How did he find out? To-morrow? What infernal nonsense! I don't believe a word of it," etc.

The young man bent still lower — looked furtively at the officers — and in an inaudible whisper poured another message into Burton's ear.

My host gave a little start and turned a trifle pale.

"The devil you say! Better come to my room, then, to-night at twelve."

"Anything up?" I asked after the man had gone, noticing the change in Burton's manner.

"Well, yes. My assistant tells me that my last letter has been overhauled this side of the frontier, and that orders for my arrest will be signed to-morrow. I don't believe it. But you can't tell, — these people are fools enough to do anything. If I knew which of my letters had reached our office I wouldn't care; but I haven't seen our paper since my first dispatches appeared, more than a month ago."

"That needn't worry you. I have every one of them in my bag at the hotel, and every issue of your paper since you arrived here. I knew I was coming, and I wanted to be posted."

Burton looked at me in open astonishment.

"You!"

"Certainly. Come to my room; get them in five minutes."

"Well, that paralyzes me! Here I have been stranded for news and blocked for weeks by these brigands who rob my mail, and here you pick me up in the streets and haul everything I want out of your carpet-bag! Don't ever put that in a story, for nobody would ever believe it. Give me a cigarette."

I opened my case, and as I handed him its contents my eyes rested on a man watching us intently. He was sitting at the officers' table. With the flaring of Burton's match his face came into full relief.

It was my friend of the morning.

"There he is again," I blurted out.

"Who?" said Burton, without moving.

"The man in the Turkish café, — the one who ordered the soldiers around. Who is he?"

Burton never moved a muscle of his face except to blow rings over his coffee-cup.

"A mean-looking hound in a slouch hat, with rat-terrier eyes, bushy beard, and a bad-fitting cloak?"

"Yes," said I, comparing the description over his shoulder.

"Why! that's my shadow, — a delicate attention bestowed on me by the prefect. He thinks I don't know him, but I fool him every day. I got two columns out last night from under his very nose, — right at this table. The waiter carried them off in a napkin, and my man nabbed them outside."

"A spy?"

"No; a shadow, a night-hawk. For nearly two months this fellow has never taken his eyes off me, and yet he has never seen me look him in the face. Come, these people are getting too sociable."

In an instant we were in the street, and in three minutes had entered my hotel. Leaving Burton in the hall, I mounted the broad staircase, went straight to my room, picked up my pocket sketch-book, and thrust the " clippings " into my inside pocket.

When I regained the corridor outside my door the man in the slouch hat was just ahead of me on his way downstairs !

Smothering my astonishment, — I had left him sitting in the garden five minutes before, — I followed slowly, matching my steps to his, and turning over in my mind whether it would be best to swallow the clippings or drop them over the balusters.

I could see Burton below, standing near the door, absorbed in an Orient express time-table tacked to the wall. (I was to leave for Constantinople the next day.) He must have heard our footsteps, but he never turned his head.

The man reached the hall floor, — I was five steps behind, — stood within ten feet of Burton, and began striking matches for a cigar which was still burning.

I decided instantly.

" Oh, Burton," I called out, " I found the

sketch-book. See what I did here yesterday ; " and I ran rapidly over the leaves, noting as I turned, "The Jews' Quarter," "Minaret of Bania-bashie," "Ox-Team down by the Bazaar," etc.

The man lingered, and I could feel him looking over my shoulder. Then the glass door clicked, and he disappeared.

Burton raised his hand warningly.

" Where did you pick *him* up ? "

" Outside my door."

" Keyhole business, eh ? Did you get them ? "

I touched my inside pocket.

" Good," and he slipped the package of clippings under his waistcoat.

The next morning I found this note tucked under my door : —

The game is up. Meet me at station at twelve.   BURTON.

Five minutes before the appointed hour my traps were heaped up in one corner of the waiting-room.

I confess to a certain degree of anxiety as I waited in the station, both on my own account and on his. I was unable to understand how the night-hawk could have reached my chamber door ahead of me unless he had sailed over the roof and dropped down the chimney, and I was equally willing to admit that something besides a desire to see me safely in bed had induced him to keyhole my movements. Perhaps his sudden disappearance through the glass door was, after all, only preparatory to his including me in the attentions he was about to pay to Burton.

When the exact hour arrived, and the Orient express direct for Philippopolis and Constantinople rolled into the depot, and still Burton did not appear, I began to realize the absurdity of waiting for a convict at the main entrance. Burton of course would be chained to two soldiers and placed in a baggage-van, or perhaps be shackled around the ankles like Voyvoda and lifted out of a cart by his waistband. The yard was the place to find him.

I made my way between the two door-guards, who eyed me in a manner that convinced me that I was under surveillance and would most likely catch both balls in the vicinity of my collar-button if I attempted to move out of range.

But there was nothing in the yard except empty cars and a squad of raw recruits sitting on their bundles awaiting transportation, and so I tried the boulevard side again.

No Burton.

Just as I was about to give him up for lost, and had begun turning over in my mind what my duty might be as a man and an American, a fresh cloud of dust blew through the open door, and a cab pulled up. From this emerged a pair of leather gaiters followed by two legs in check trousers, a hand with white wristbands and English gloves, and last the cool, unruffled face of Burton himself.

"Yes, I am late, but I have been up all night dictating. You got my note, I see. I go as far with you as Philippopolis, where I get out to reach the Pomuk Highlands. You remember I told you about that old brigand chief, Achmet Aga, who rules a province of forty square miles and pays tribute to no one, not even the Sultan. You know he murders everybody who crosses his line without his permission. Well, I am going to interview him."

This was said in one breath and with as much ease of manner and indifference to surroundings as if the man with a slouch hat had been an idle dream instead of an active reality.

"But what about your arrest, Burton ? I expected" —

"Expected what — dungeons ? Nonsense. I simply went out on my balcony last night before I crawled into bed, sneezed, and called out in French to my man inside to pack my bag for this train. That satisfied my shadow, for all he wants is to get me out of the way. Don't worry; the dog will be here to see us off."

Burton was right. That ugly face was the last that peered at us as we rolled out of the station.

Six hours later I left my new friend at Philippopolis with a regret I cannot explain, but with an exacted promise to meet me in Constantinople a week later, where we would enjoy the Turks together.

The week passed, and another, and then a third, and still no sign of Burton. I had begun to wonder whether, after all, the brigand chief had not served him as he had done his predecessors, when this letter, dated Sofia, reached me, —

"Just returned from the mountains. Spent a most delightful week with Achmet Aga, who kissed me on both cheeks when I left, and gave me a charm against fire and sword blessed by all the wise women of the clan. Would have joined you before, but had to hurry back here for the opening of the Sobranje.

307

A BULGARIAN OPERA BOUFFE

"Stamboloff's party carried the day by a small majority, and the town is full of his men, including the prince, who opened parliament here yesterday."

THE END

www.ingramcontent.com/pod-product-compliance
Lightning Source LLC
Chambersburg PA
CBHW030243030726
47493CB00023B/572